Also by Scott Geisel

JACKSON FLINT MYSTERY NOVELS
Fair Game
Water to Bind

OTHER STORIES
Cinderbox Road & Other Stories
Masquerade
Escape Velocity

MILLER KNEW

An Appalachian Noir and Suspense Story

Scott Geisel

Fox&
Possum
PUBLISHING

Thanks and appreciation to Macy Reynolds, Laurie Martt, Luan Heit, and Dan Rudolf. You are forever the all-stars.

And special thanks and love to Pam, who reminded me that this story lay half-written in my desk drawer and urged me to finish it because she wanted to know what happened.

PART 1

1

MILLER KNEW.

He knew when he heard the whine of the truck coming through the woods that there would be trouble.

Virginia hillfolk had been navigating this rural country since Europeans began claiming lands here. The early homesteaders had pushed into the hills to scratch out their lives away from the prying eyes of neighbors and the government. Later, hillfolk cut rutted and muddy paths up to the iron veins that fed the stone blast furnaces down in the river valley. They pushed rock ore by hand over switchback trails that slithered and bumped through the trees, the trails appearing and disappearing and reappearing as rain and weather and neglect and need dictated.

When outsiders came later for the coal and timber, hillfolk worked the mines and the sawmills and drove the trucks that pulled the fuel and wood from the land. They hauled the bounty down to the roadways and to the barges on the river that snaked away through the mountains. Their work was fueled and their troubles were tempered by whiskey the men cooked in stills forged from copper and pots.

And when the mines closed and the lumber was hauled away and what was left of the forests and scrub inevitably began to reclaim the abandoned timber and coal roads, the hillfolk remained as they had been. Enclaves became small towns, communities that had seen booms and been forgotten, generations of families that held on to remote, ancestral lands. Lands they believed were theirs by right and had always been, despite the history that came before them.

Miller was hillfolk. He'd grown up bouncing along these nearly impassable backways on the truck seat next to his pa, hunting, poaching, foraging, and generally keeping their distance from others. Miller's pa had given him the wheel of the truck at fourteen, and now at sixteen he could ease the old truck through its gears and over the ruts and ridges and wash-outs that threatened to swallow a vehicle or sluice it down into a ravine.

The sound of the truck moving toward them now was wrong. Miller knew it was a truck. Only a vehicle with good clearance underneath could have made it this far, and he'd never seen anything but a truck back in these woods. But the timbre he heard was wrong. The truck revved when it should have lugged, whined when it should have ground. The gearing was wrong, the clutch work sloppy.

It meant either teenagers from town come up here to have some fun that would probably turn into trouble if they could find it, or a hillfolk who had gotten into his bottle and was slipping the gears, or worse. Miller hoped it was teenagers.

He called to his sister. "Jeannie, get in the truck."

Jeannie was with him gathering wood to take back and cut for the potbelly stove they were using more and more now that the nights were getting cold. She was attempting to roll a length of hardwood nearly as thick as her narrow waist to the back of the truck.

"Jeannie, get in the truck."

She looked at Miller and swiped a lock of hair back under her knitted hat. "What?"

"Didn't you hear me? I said to get in the truck."

Jeannie scanned the woods with a twist of her neck. "Why?"

Miller cocked an ear and pointed a finger. "You hear that?"

She grinned. "So what? You think someone's gonna try to take our firewood? There's plenty." She kicked the length of maple she'd been struggling with.

Miller left the chunk of walnut he had been dragging and came to his little sister and laid a hand on her arm. "It's best not to be seen."

Jeannie laughed and pushed Miller's hand away. "You sound like daddy did."

She said it with finality. Like daddy did. But he doesn't do now. As if she knew their father wasn't coming back. Miller held a begrudging admiration of his sister for that. She was probably right. Pa had only been gone a couple of weeks, but they'd heard nothing and Miller had a tight spot in his chest that said he expected the worst.

"Pa was right. We don't know who they are or what they want. You should get in the truck."

Jeannie groaned. "Probably just out joyriding. Or shooting guns or poaching deer. Like everybody does." She nudged the edge of the limb with a booted toe. "Are you going to help me with this or what?"

Miller grinned. "Or what."

"Doofus."

"Goofy."

"Mental midget."

Miller laughed. "Good one. That's new." He bent to grab the end of wood Jeannie had toted and grunted as he lifted it to the back of the truck and pushed. "Think you could help here, or are you not going to use any of that heat I'm going to put into the house with this?"

Jeannie swiped at Miller's arm. "You saying I'm not doing my share?"

He pushed again on the log and it scraped farther up into the bed of the truck. "Well, you are kind of a runt. There's only so much can be expected of you."

Actually, the opposite was true. Miller was amazed and impressed by the way his sister had been bucking up under the circumstances, just the two of them in the house, with both their ma and pa gone now. He felt both protective and proud of Jeannie, and something else that he couldn't quite put a name to, a kind of brotherly love he hadn't thought possible before.

They lifted another log together and set one end onto the back of the truck. Miller climbed into the bed to pull the wood up. He stopped to listen to the sound of the approaching truck again. "I still think you should—"

Just then a pick-up older and rustier than theirs crested a rise in the woods and Miller let his words drop.

Jeannie looked surprised. "They're coming over here. Why are they coming over here?"

Miller grunted, and the truck pulled closer and stopped a couple dozen yards behind them. Two men about as old as his pa, in their forties, got out. They were skinny and looked dirty, and the driver came in front of their truck and started on a long piss he aimed in Miller's direction. The man wobbled a bit on his heels, and he was close enough that Miller could see a gnarled cut over his eye that looked like it wasn't healing right, and a black spot in his gums where he might have lost a tooth.

Jeannie looked away. Miller tried not to notice, but noticed, that the man's penis was loose and flopped and he sprinkled awkwardly as he finished. Miller cut his eyes to Jeannie. "Get in the truck."

The driver zipped and said, "Now hold on there. You two're stealing our firewood."

Jeannie moved toward the truck cab. The second man took quick steps toward her and reached out a hand. "Wait."

Jeannie stopped. Miller was still in the bed of the truck standing among the logs and limbs. His eyes moved over sizes and shapes, searching. "You can have it," he said. "Ain't nothin' but deadfall anyway."

The man close to Jeannie opened his jacket to show the polished white handle of a pistol tucked into his belt. "That ain't the point," he said. "This here's our wood you got."

A bottle had appeared in the driver's hand. He took a long drink, then raised the bottle again and took another. He looked at Miller and pointed the neck of the bottle at Jeannie. "That your kin?"

Miller took a step toward the rear of the truck bed and the man with the gun reached to his belt and said, "Stand right there, boy."

Miller recognized this man. He'd seen him with his pa sometimes, when pa was running bootleg to the bars down in the flatlands. And he recognized on both men the familiar stinking drunk of boys who had learned to drink young and become men who made a life of drinking. Men who could drink for two days straight and get mean enough for trouble they would not remember or regret when they sobered up, if they sobered up.

Miller took another step toward the back of the truck. "She's thirteen." His mind went to the rifle behind the seat in the cab.

The men looked to each other. The driver nodded. "That sounds about right."

Jeannie was almost fourteen. She reminded Miller of it whenever he called her his baby sister. But this time Jeannie stood hunched inside of her coat and didn't correct him.

The men stepped toward Miller's sister.

Miller jumped from the truck bed and the man with the gun slapped him hard with a backhand. Miller tasted blood and felt rage and came up with a fist, but the man stepped in and blocked the jab and then Miller felt another blow to his jaw, and another and another, and they came too fast for him to stop them and he went down.

"Don't make this harder than it has to be, boy," the man said. He reached out and took hold of Jeannie's arm.

Run, Miller thought. She should have run.

The man pulled Jeannie close to him and said, "Y'all

have to be taught a lesson about taking what ain't yours."
He laughed and it turned into something hacking from his
lungs and he cocked his head to the side and spat.

The driver approached them and cackled. "Girl will do
fine. She'll learn quick."

Miller raised himself up. The man with the gun kicked him
hard in the shin and Miller went down again. "Stay down.
Boys don't supposed to be messin' in men's doings." He
pointed to the truck door. "Get in there and wait 'til it's over."

Miller tried to signal his sister with his eyes, but Jeannie
did not look back at him. Her eyes were steeled on the man
who had a hold on her.

The man cooed to Jeannie. "Don't worry none, now. It
ain't nothin' but what hillfolk been doing since they was
hillfolk." He laughed again and it turned into something
choked in his lungs again and it cut the laugh off. He squared
his gaze on Jeannie. "My daddy taught me when I was not
much older'n you. And on a pretty little thing like you."

Jeannie's face was hard, but Miller saw a shine in her eye
that he knew was a teardrop she was fighting to keep from
leaking out.

The man cut a look to Miller, crouched beside the truck.
"I'd'a thought you'd know by now what it means to be a
man."

Miller knew. He'd seen men like this all his life. They
were grown but they weren't men. Not like he believed was
right for a man to be.

Jeannie fought back as the man tugged her away from
the truck toward the mottled shelter of the woods. "Don't."
Her eyes could not hold back the wet in them now.

The driver followed, and as he passed the truck Miller raised up through the pain in his shin and in his jaw where he had been kicked and punched. He reached into the bed and grasped the garden shovel they had tucked there and swung it from the handle. He swung hard and fast and the man had turned to Miller so the blade of the shovel came up under his chin at a sharp angle and cut a dark chunk of meat from his throat and the side of his face.

The man screamed and grabbed for his face and fell to his knees, but Miller ignored him. He closed fast on the other who had a hold on his sister.

The man let go of Jeannie and she darted away. He turned to Miller and squared himself and reached to his waist for the gun. But Miller was already on him and he had the shovel going, but he was too close too fast to swing. He let the shovel go and reached desperately for the gun, pressing against the cold metal to turn the barrel away.

Their eyes met and Miller saw fear and drunkenness in the other's whites. Then they fell together and Miller came down on top of the man and their hands closed and the gun between them boomed once.

The shock of the discharge rang up Miller's arm, and the echo of the explosion raced through the hills.

Miller let go of the man and the gun and raised himself. A bright red bloom gushed from the man's chest.

The man behind Miller whose neck had been dug with the shovel gurgled and choked. The man with the hole in his chest clutched at the wound and whispered, "Help…"

Miller did nothing. He waited, and in another minute or two both men lay quiet and unmoving.

Miller looked out at the woods and the rutted land and hills. He looked back at the men and felt something in himself he hadn't known before, a thing that coursed through his psyche like a dark wave. He spoke over the men's bodies. "It ain't nothing but what hillfolk been doing since they was hillfolk."

Then he spat. "Hillfolk be damned."

2

MILLER HEARD boots crunching on brittle leaves. The cold blew through him, and he felt himself as if one of the dead, swirling leaves, falling into a dark and endless winter.

The sound grew closer, then Jeannie was there at his side. He tried to hug her but she didn't want that and pulled away. He let her go. His hands were shaking, but from rage or something else, he didn't know. "How much did you see?"

"I saw it."

He studied his sister. Her eyes were dry but her face was twisted in a way he didn't know. "These weren't men," he said.

She pulled some strands of hair from her face. Her eyes flitted over the dead men, then away. "It had to be done. Daddy would'a done it."

Miller knew it was true but he wasn't sure he liked the connection she was making. He grunted. "You OK?"

"I dunno. I guess I'll have to be."

Miller thought about that and he figured it was a pretty good answer.

Jeannie looked up at Miller's face. "He busted your lip."

Miller reached and touched the wet spot, the swollen lump. "Yeah, some."

"It ain't no worse than what daddy ever done."

Miller guessed it wasn't, and he pushed the toe of his boot against the man with the hole in his chest. The dead man didn't move. Miller toed him harder and he still didn't move, so he picked up the shovel and went to the other dead man.

Jeannie followed him. The shovel head was heavy with blood. "We'll have to rinse the shovel," he said.

Jeannie let out a stifled giggle.

Miller turned to her. "It ain't funny."

Jeannie's face dropped. "I know. I just don't know how I'm supposed to act."

He nodded. "That's OK. Neither do I."

Miller toed the other man and he didn't move either. He placed the shovel into the truck bed and came back and took hold of the man's feet. When he started to drag the body, the man's coat bunched up around his torso and leaves piled up at his shoulders.

"What're you doing?" Jeannie said.

Miller stopped pulling. "We've got to get rid of them."

Jeannie's head bobbed back and forth. "We got to call the law."

Miller let go of the body and came to his sister. Her face was scrunched and her eyes were tight and her head was still moving back and forth. He wished he could just send her

home. Wished she didn't have to be here, that men didn't
have to be the way these men had been, that his father was
here to do what had to be done so he wouldn't have to. That
they didn't have to be here scrounging deadfall like that in
the first place. That they were different people and lived different lives in a different place.

Miller took Jeannie's hand and looked into her eyes.
"Listen."

Her chin came up.

"If we call the law, they'll come and ask questions.
They'll come out to the house."

Jeannie's eyes focused on Miller and widened.

"They'll want to talk to ma and pa." He squeezed his
sister's hand tighter. "And ma and pa won't be there."

Jeannie's eyes looked wet again, and Miller let go of her
hand and she wiped at them. "They'll take us away. If they
find out we're living alone, they won't let us stay."

Jeannie sniffed and her shoulders bounced once. "OK."

"We've talked about this."

"I know."

Miller looked into his sister's eyes. She looked back
at him and her shoulders came up. "I'm OK." Then she
stepped over to the body and reached down and took hold
of the man's coat sleeves.

Miller held up a hand. "No."

Jeannie lifted higher on the dead man's sleeves. "We
can't waste no time. It's going to get dark."

They dragged the body to the men's truck and they lifted the weight of him into the back. Then they went back for
the other, and when they had him up in the bed of the truck

Miller got the tarp from theirs and spread it over the men and tied it down.

It was hard work. The bodies were loose and sagged and they weren't easy to lift. When they were done it was nearly dark and had gotten colder, though the heat of the work had warmed them.

Miller looked in the men's truck for the keys and when they weren't there he had to scoot under the tarp and fish into the dead man's pocket for them.

He climbed down to his sister. "You'll have to drive our truck home, then come back out and get me."

"Why would I do that?"

"It's best you're not part of what comes next."

Jeannie didn't argue.

Miller's mind was clear enough that he was grateful she didn't ask what he would do with the men. It was an ugly thing he faced, and Miller tried not to let his mind recognize it any more than he had to. He hoped his sister could do the same, but he'd have to worry about her later. Right now, they had to move.

Miller reached into his own pocket and came out with the keys to their truck and gave them to Jeannie. "You got to be real careful. We'll wait until it's all the way dark to come out of the woods to the road. You drive real steady, right at the speed limit. Keep your focus. Stop where you're supposed to stop and drive like I showed you."

"I will."

"Wait an hour after you get home, then start back out to get me."

"Where will you be?"

He thought about it. "I'll come back to the road where it turns in here. He pointed to the dirt track they'd come in on. "Make it two hours."

"Whyn't I just come get you?"

"It's best you don't know any more." Jeannie looked down, and Miller saw the fear in her. "Maybe I should just walk home."

"No, I can do it."

"Be better if you just go home."

"It'd take you all night to walk. In the cold and dark."

Miller hesitated. "I don't want you driving, after…"

Jeannie moved around him toward their truck. "I can do it."

Miller knew she could. He didn't want her to have to.

"What should I do with the wood?"

"Just leave it in the back."

Jeannie's eyes were wide in a way that Miller didn't understand. He wanted again to hug her, but she'd already pushed him away. "Unless you want to try and unload some of it."

"It'll give me something to do."

Something to keep her mind off what Miller had done, and what he was about to do. What the men had tried to do to her.

Jeannie stopped with the truck door held open and looked back at Miller. "What are you going to do with their truck when it's done?"

He watched the set of Jeannie's jaw, the line of her leg and boot poised on the step up into the truck. He wasn't sure any of this was right. He set his own jaw and said, "Same as with them."

3

MILLER DROVE them home after Jeannie came back to pick him up. It was late when they got back, and the house was dark and cold. Their short-haired mutt, Bailey, lay curled beside the potbelly stove, waiting for someone to come over and put wood in it and heat it up.

Neither of them did, and the house stayed cold and they went to bed under their heavy covers and tried to sleep.

Pictures kept playing in Miller's head and he had dreams he didn't like. He got up twice in the night to look in on Jeannie. Bailey had gotten into bed with her and was curled up at her side with his head tucked under a scrap of blanket. Jeannie lay still and breathed shallow and evenly and looked all right.

Before dawn, Miller got up and turned on the light under the counter in the kitchen and put two logs in the potbelly, enough to take some of the chill off the room.

They had a furnace with gas heat, but the furnace was old and needed repairs to the heat exchanger, and gas cost money. Pa had shut off the gas line and wouldn't let them use the furnace because he said it was too dangerous with the carbon monoxide that might come out. It would be better to replace the whole thing. But pa was gone and it had gotten cold and the furnace was still broken, so they chopped wood.

Bailey came out and sniffed around the kitchen floor for a scrap. When he didn't find one, he went out through the breezeway that had been enclosed with plywood, and Miller heard him push through the dog door at the far end.

Pa didn't like the dog door. He'd rather let a dog mostly fend for himself, feed him just enough to keep him close and discourage critters and visitors, be there when he wanted the dog for hunting. But he'd relented when Jeannie couldn't stand the thought of Bailey outside alone and had begged pa to let him in.

The compromise had been the dog door at the end of the breezeway. Bailey's door was covered with thick scraps of carpet and opened into the woodpile under the lean-to, and it was disguised enough that even if someone saw the dog scuffling around there he might not realize there was a door.

Pa would have closed off the kitchen door to the back breezeway when it got cold to keep the heat in, leaving Bailey to the whims of whoever wanted to let him in or out or not. But with ma and pa gone, Miller and Jeannie liked having Bailey both inside with them and outside prowling, so they kept the breezeway door propped open enough that the dog could get through.

The room began to heat up, and in a few minutes Bailey came back in and turned in circles beside the stove and lay down and tucked his head onto his paws.

Miller made cornmeal cakes in the iron pan and set out peanut butter and molasses and an apple on the table and waited.

In a little while, Jeannie got up and came out and sat at the table. Miller watched her. "How you doing?"

Jeannie's eyes came up, then went back down. Her shoulders rolled once. "I keep seeing them."

He nodded. "It'll get easier. You have to let your mind go off it. It'll start to fade."

Jeannie didn't say anything for a minute and then she looked up. "That doesn't help much now."

Miller took a breath before he spoke. "I know it doesn't feel that way, but it does help. Knowing it will pass makes it easier now when it's still fresh. You have to think like that— think ahead."

Jeannie sat still. "I don't know if I can."

"You can." Miller forked corn cakes onto a plate and pushed them toward her. "The best thing is to do normal things. It'll take your mind off remembering."

She squinted at the corn cakes. "How do you know?"

Miller shook his head. The memories were there, tucked away but always close. Pa had been a hard man to live with. "It's not good to remember everything."

Jeannie looked at her plate, looked around the kitchen, looked at the potbelly stove and the stack of wood beside it that would always disappear too fast. Looked at Miller. "Things ain't looked very normal around here for a while."

Miller felt something grip the corners of his mouth and tug at them, and it pulled against the cut and swollen spot on his lip. He set his jaw. "Normal as we can."

Jeannie held her look on him. "Your face looks a little better."

"Yeah." He'd checked in the mirror when he got up. The lip looked better, but there was a purple smear under his jaw, and oddly mottled lines high on his cheek bone that would look like an imprint from fingers or knuckles to anyone who recognized them. Folks around here would. Other blows had landed higher on his head when he went down, but Miller wasn't concerned about those. They were above his hairline and wouldn't show.

Miller and Jeannie ate, but neither of them was very interested in the food. When they were finished, Miller wrapped the leftover corn cakes in foil and put them in the fridge. They could eat them tonight with the chili he planned to make. He would use the beans he'd taken from the food drive barrel in Johnson's Market when no one was looking.

They had a little money and could buy some food, but Miller was tight with what they had. Stealing wasn't something he'd been brought up to do, but Miller had seen his pa do it with cigarettes and candy bars and such, and it was a lesson not taught but easily learned. Besides, if folks in town knew the situation they were in, he and Jeannie would be getting food from the barrel anyway.

Miller scraped the bottom of the iron skillet and wiped it with a towel and set it on a cold burner on the stove, then he started in on the breakfast dishes and called over his shoulder to Jeannie. "It's getting late. You best be getting ready for school."

Jeannie appeared at his elbow and picked up a clean plate and wiped it dry. She set it on the shelf over the sink with the other clean plates and cups. "I ain't going today."

Miller washed another plate and set it on the drain board. "We need to go."

"You said we need to do normal things. School ain't normal. Washing plates and picking up the house and cooking food and splitting firewood is normal. School ain't."

Miller finished with the dishes and let the water drain from the sink. "You might be right about school. But it's what we need to do today."

"No way. Not today."

"It's the best thing. Nobody will wonder where we are, and no one will call home looking for us."

"They don't never call if you miss. They just check you off their list and figure it's up to your ma and pa whether they want to make you go or not."

He dried his hands on a towel. "I know it's not easy, but we have to go. It'll take our mind off things."

Jeannie stuck her lip out and leveled her eyes on Miller's. "You ain't mamma or daddy."

"No, but I got pull. Now go and get ready."

She turned, then looked back over her shoulder as she walked away. "Doofus."

"Goofy."

She grinned. "Peach fuzz." She rubbed a hand on her chin where Miller's imaginary hair would be.

He snapped the towel at her. It missed and she swatted it away and said, "I'll hurry so you'll be sure and have time to shave." She rubbed her chin again where neither she nor Miller had hair.

He wound the towel again for another swat, but Jeannie had gone.

While she was getting ready, he turned on the TV with the volume almost off and looked at the news. There was nothing about missing men or a missing truck. He hadn't expected there would be so soon, but his mind wouldn't let it go until he'd checked.

He left the TV playing and went over to look through the window toward the neighbors. The Jacksons had lived next door to them his whole life, but he'd never really gotten to know them. Old man Jackson didn't like Miller's father, and Miller suspected the feeling had been mutual, though his father had mostly just ignored the house next door.

They were the only two houses together here, set back from the road on a shared dirt drive that split, with them on the left and the Jacksons to the right. Behind them the terrain dropped into a shallow ravine and a creek that snaked away through the hills. Beyond that the land rose sharply and raggedly.

Their house was three rooms, depending on who was telling it. There was a tiny bedroom and living room. A kitchen big enough for the potbelly stove and a table. Outside there was a well and a pump and an electric line that sagged through the trees and snaked down through the soffit into the house.

When Miller and Jeannie had grown too old to sleep in the makeshift beds in the living room, pa scavenged plywood and lumber from a tear-down and used that to enclose the porch at the back of the house. It made two rooms big enough for a bed each and a door that would close.

Pa said that made it a five-room house, but Ma held that it was still three rooms and an all-weather addition. The insulation was thin in Miller and Jeannie's rooms and there were no ducts, so they were exposed to the heat and cold. Miller figured Ma's version told it about right.

He leaned close to the window at the front of the house. With most of the leaves down from the trees now he could see the Jackson house next door, could make out the light in the kitchen window and the truck parked out front, could see their front porch and if there was someone sitting out on it or not. He wondered now how much the Jacksons paid attention to what was going on at his own house. Whether they'd grown suspicious about ma and pa yet.

Jeannie came out wearing jeans and a sweater, and Miller handed her a paper lunch sack. She looked inside. "What's in it?"

"Peanut butter."

She made a face. "We had peanut butter for breakfast."

"There's an apple too."

"We had an apple for breakfast too."

Miller grunted. "If I gave you eggs and bacon and potatoes every day to eat would you complain about that?"

Jeannie grinned. "Let's try it and find out."

Miller shook his head and stuffed his own lunch into his backpack. "There's something else in the bottom too. A surprise."

Jeannie peeked into her bag.

"Don't look yet. Save it for later and it'll be better."

She reluctantly rolled the top of the bag back down. "Doofus."

"Wait until you see what it is and you might be calling me something different."

It was a pack of cupcakes. He'd swiped a box of them when he took the beans and some other things from the food barrel. It wasn't something they needed, and it had been a risk stuffing the long box of cupcakes under his jacket, but Miller was glad now that he'd done it. It gave him and Jeannie a good thing to talk about. A normal thing.

They went out and down the porch steps and Jeannie headed for the truck.

"No, we'll take the bus."

"I don't like taking the bus."

"Neither do I, but it'll save on gas. And it's better for today."

She stooped her shoulders and walked like it was a heavy load he'd laid on her, but they went.

4

MILLER STEELED himself to make it through the day.

The bus ride to school had gone okay. Mr. Blackman, the bus driver—which was weird, because he was a black man and one of the very few Miller had ever seen around here—opened the bus doors and as they climbed up he said, "I've not seen you two at this stop much lately."

"No, sir," Miller said. "Pa's been droppin' us off some, or sometimes we walk."

It was a lie that Miller knew Mr. Blackman had probably heard a lot, but the bus driver accepted it now with a nod. "Long walk."

"Yes, sir, but we ain't had much better to do."

Miller looked down as he walked past Mr. Blackman, but he knew the man saw the marks on his face and said nothing.

The ride was quiet but got gradually louder as they picked up more people. Jeannie sat near the middle talking to some other girls, and Miller kept to himself in the back of the bus.

The bus climbed up and down the dips and rolls in the road and stopped at little clumps of houses like where Miller lived, but most of them had more—six or eight or ten homes together in a stretch.

Miller wondered where Mr. Blackman lived and if he had kids, and if he did, where they went to school. He'd not seen more than a few black kids in his classes, and he was pretty sure none of them were Mr. Blackman's, but he didn't really know.

When the bus lumbered to a stop outside of the regional school, Jeannie followed the girls she'd been sitting with toward the junior high wing and Miller went to the high school side. He skipped his locker and went straight to homeroom and sat at his desk with his head down and his hand over the bruises and the cut on his lip. He was quiet and kept to himself. He didn't have to wonder what the others would think about the way he looked. He knew they'd figure his pa had done it.

Things went all right until he got to Mr. Ellsburg's American History class. He took his seat in the back by the windows and wasn't paying attention. Then about halfway through class he heard two boys he knew but didn't talk to much whispering about another boy he didn't know who had his head on his desk and was sleeping. Miller cocked an ear and heard, "His sister told me their dad didn't come home last night and their mom about went crazy and kept them up all night frettin'."

That turned Miller's thoughts to the night his own pa hadn't come home. The next day when he still wasn't there, and the slow realization that it was just him and Jeannie now. That pa might come home again or he might not. That he couldn't see a future that wasn't clouded with worry about what would come next.

Miller wondered if the boy with his head down on his desk had been thinking the same things. Then he wondered if the boy's father could be one of the men from last night, and images from the woods and what he'd done after crashed through his head. His heart felt like it had shrunk to a tight little walnut in his chest.

Then he heard Mr. Ellsburg.

"Albert Brenning, did you hear me? Will you answer the question, please?"

It felt like the walls had moved in and everyone was looking at him. He opened his eyes, and they *were* looking at him.

Then he heard the snickers. Someone whispered, "Bert."

He hated it when they called him Bert. *Hey, Bert, where's Ernie? Where's your rubber ducky?*

In grade school he'd fought back by taking a swing at whoever said it, but that was what they wanted. Later he'd worked hard at trying to get everyone to call him by his middle name. Miller.

But Mr. Ellsburg couldn't be trained.

"No, sir," Miller said. "Can you ask it again?"

Mr. Ellsburg made a big show of sighing and screwed up his face like dealing with Miller was a burden no teacher deserved. "Will you tell the class, please, who was the French marquis known for helping the colonies during the American Revolution, and who has a statue and a park named for himself in front of the White House? Can you do that for us, Bert?"

Miller clenched his fists. He breathed. And then it came out. "I sure as hell don't know, but if I ever get to Washington. I'll be sure and look that up for you, Leslie."

He and the others all knew that Mr. Ellsburg was sensitive about his first name, and they'd been smart enough to only make fun of that behind his back.

Mr. Ellsburg's face screwed up tight and he spat back at Miller, "You can go straight to the main office and tell them you need to sit there and wait for me to come down after class. We'll go in and see Mr. Jenkins together."

Jenkins was the principal. This wouldn't be the first time Miller had been sent to his office.

Some of the other boys in the back of the room *oohed* as Miller picked up his things. Someone whispered "Bert" again.

As he walked past Mr. Ellsburg's desk, Miller said, "I look forward to that, Leslie."

Mr. Ellsburg's eyes flashed wide and he slapped an open palm down hard on his desk, but Miller was gone.

He didn't go to the office. He didn't meet Mr. Jenkins. Miller walked to his locker and dumped his books in and went right past the office and out the front doors. He hiked across the field beside the school and into the path through a copse that led to the road where it switched back away from the school and into the hills.

It was a long walk home, like Mr. Blackman had said. Nearly five miles by road. But that would be quicker than the more direct route rambling over the hills and through the underbrush.

A few cars passed Miller as he walked. He ignored them and navigated to the weedy open fields away from the road as much as he could.

He ate his lunch and thought about how he and Jeannie were going to get by until either ma or pa came back, if either of them ever did come back. He didn't like the way that made him feel, so he let his mind wonder. He shouldn't have. It went to the night before, and the look in Jeannie's eyes when one of the men had grabbed hold of her.

He walked and whistled and tried to make his mind go to nothing as much as possible.

When he came within sight of home it was deep into the afternoon. The sun angled sharply across the sky and lit up the front of the house.

There was a man standing on the porch looking in the window.

5

MILLER SLOWED his steps and raised a hand over his eyes against the sun to get a better look. He figured they'd come to take him and Jeannie away.

But the man on the porch looked wrong. He was wearing jeans and dirty boots. Flannel jacket, stringy hair that almost reached his shoulders. There was no suit or even a nice shirt and jacket or a briefcase, and a dusty pick-up was parked at the fork in the driveways.

Miller picked up his pace and scanned the trees behind the house. Where was Bailey?

As he approached the steps, the man turned quickly from the window and looked surprised. Miller closed to the porch and stopped at the bottom step. "Pa won't like strangers lookin' in the window."

The man's face twisted and he stepped awkwardly back from Miller. "Now hold on." He held up a hand. "Is your daddy home?"

"Might be. He might be sleepin'. Might be workin.'

When he wakes or comes home I'll tell him you was here looking for him."

"No, hang on." The hand went up again. "You don't have to do that."

Miller took the first step up onto the porch. "Who did you say you was?" He put a finger and thumb into his mouth and let out a loud, high-pitched trilling whistle for Bailey. "You seen my dog?"

The man's shoulders dropped and his head bobbed slightly. "Look, I don't even wanna be here. My wife sent me." He cocked his gaze at Miller. "You know Rubylee Slocum over at the school? Your sister and her are friends. Jeannie's been comin' over to the house?"

Rubylee was one of the girls from the bus. Miller knew that Jeannie talked with her and they were probably friends. And Rubylee had a brother, Dundee, who was Miller's age though he didn't know him well. Miller nodded once, tightly. "Yeah."

There was a rustling from beyond the corner of the house and Bailey came running from around the woodpile. He stopped at the bottom of the steps behind Miller and barked sharply at the other man.

"She's my daughter," the man said. "I'm Jud Slocum. Rubylee and Jeannie are friends and I—"

Bailey had lowered himself behind Miller and was baring his teeth up at the man on the porch.

Slocum lifted a heavy boot in the direction of Bailey. "Don't make me hurt your dog. That ain't why I come here." Bailey did not advance, and Slocum lowered his boot back to the porch floorboards. "I didn't come here to hurt nobody."

Miller regarded Slocum for a long beat, then he spoke Bailey's name to calm the dog. When Bailey had quieted some, Miller returned his look to Slocum. "Why are you here? Something happen to Rubylee?" Then his heart grew tighter. "Did something happen to Jeannie?"

"No. No." Slocum was shaking his head. "It ain't like that. I come here because…"

Miller waited while Slocum ran the fingers of one hand through his gnarled hair. "My wife made me come." He sighed quickly. "You've got to understand, I wouldn't be here if she hadn't insisted I check in."

Miller folded his arms across his chest. "Check in?"

"Let's just forget it."

Miller took a step back from the porch and gave Bailey a push with his toe to move the dog over behind him.

Slocum moved forward but stopped before he came down the steps and said, "My wife said she thought she saw something. She wanted to make sure everything was all right with Jeannie and you and your pa."

Miller's mind went to the chili beans and canned goods and peanut butter he'd taken from the food barrel and slipped into his backpack. He tried to keep himself from asking about it, but it itched at him. Maybe it was better to know than to keep him awake at night wondering. "She saw something?"

Slocum nodded.

"What did she see?"

"I can't say." He had his hands in his pockets like all he really wanted to do was turn and go, but Slocum said, "In town. At the grocery. She wouldn't let on what it was. She just told me to look in and see you was all right."

"You've seen. We're all right."

"OK." Slocum took the first step down. "Look, I just wanted to talk to your pa. No one's seen him for a while, and with your ma…"

Miller finished it for him. "With my ma gone."

"Come on now. Everybody knows your ma run off some time ago after…"

Miller let the words hang between them.

Slocum came back to them. "After what happened."

Miller kept his voice flat so it would reveal nothing. "Ma is on an extended visit with family."

"OK," Slocum said. "We was just trying to be neighborly. People ain't been seeing your pa around, and we wanted to make sure of things."

Miller touched the side of his face, let his fingers run over the bruise and the purple outlines of fingers. He wanted Slocum to see, to think his pa had been home to do it.

Slocum did like Miller had hoped. He looked down with his eyes in a way that said he didn't like what he saw, but men here didn't ask how other men chose to raise their sons. They didn't poke their noses into others' business.

Miller said, "Pa ain't never been much for company here at the house. I don't expect he'll want you back. But I'll give him the message you was here askin' in about our welfare."

Slocum finally descended the steps. He turned at the bottom and said, "No need," and he continued to his truck and climbed in and drove away.

6

MILLER TOOK his backpack into the house and came back out with Bailey and looked at the woodpile. There were barely enough logs in the little lean-to beside the house to hide Bailey's door.

If there was a cold spell, and there likely would be one soon, it might hold them for a couple of weeks if they were stingy. A little longer if they really stretched it, but the house would be cold and uncomfortable.

Miller knew that if you intended to heat a house though the winter with wood, it was best to have the whole season cut before it got cold. When he was little, before the old used gas furnace went in, his pa had gone on what ma called a bad streak. Miller recognized that now as one of his earliest memories of the binge drinking pa had always been subject to.

They'd run out of everything during pa's bender. When the firewood was gone and the house had frozen and the pipes might burst, pa pulled himself together enough to get off the couch and cut wood late into the night by lantern. The chainsaw had roared through the hills in the dark and ma had been mortified that the neighbors knew they'd been slack and caught short, cutting into the night like that.

Miller picked up the axe and set a hunk of wood on the chopping block. Where the hell was his pa now?

He split wood. He cleaned sawdust from the chainsaw air filter and carburetor, poured fuel into the tank, and cut the pieces they'd gathered the night before. He split those and stacked them.

He tried not to think, but there was a sense in him that he needed to understand things. His ma had disappeared nearly three months before in the heat of the summer. They'd heard nothing since then. It had nearly shattered Jeannie, who couldn't bring herself to do anything for nearly a week after ma left, and then one morning she had simply shut it off. Jeannie didn't ask after that about ma, and she never mentioned ma's absence again. She moved on like things were settled. They weren't.

Pa hadn't said a word when ma disappeared. Some of her clothes were gone, but she hadn't left a note or said a thing to Miller or Jeannie. She was just gone one day.

Pa said it was so she could have time to get herself together, and he wouldn't say a word more. But pa would never do a thing around the house without ma there to poke him to do it. Miller had taken over almost right away with the cooking and dishes and cleaning, and pa had let him.

They all pretended things were normal and ma was coming back, any time. And without saying it, they all agreed that nobody would talk to anybody outside the family about it.

When pa disappeared it was less of a surprise.

Pa never had much money because pa didn't like to work. He said it was because he didn't like anyone that wasn't as smart as he was telling him what to do. But pa always had time for drinking and shooting pool with other men. He never complained about throwing in with men who had lesser talents in those areas.

Pa liked dancing in the kitchen with ma after she'd had a few drinks of his homemade shine, and he liked anything to do with a truck or a chainsaw or a shotgun. He liked complaining about what a sorry state the world was in, and why didn't Miller get off his ass and try'n do something about it?

And when his mood went dark, pa was meaner'n a possum in a sack.

Ma tried to stay out of the way and keep the peace and do what pa asked of her, and that meant staying home and keeping house and raising Miller and Jeannie. Putting dinner on the table when he was home to eat it, and even when he wasn't. Showing him some lovin' when the mood struck him.

Ma put up with it, like a lot of women Miller had seen, parents of school friends he'd been over to visit. Miller's ma always pined for more, but his pa would shake his head and say "Dammit, woman, I'd give you more if I had it. You know I would. But they ain't no more to give. There ain't no good jobs out there for a man with my skills and intelligence to work at."

Miller supposed they weren't so different from a lot of other families around here, mothers in the kitchen and fathers out somewhere or another. Except he figured the others still had at least one parent at home.

There had been no news about pa since he left. No report to the police, nothing from the neighbors, until Mr. Slocum today.

The biggest difference Miller had noticed with pa gone was that the house was more quiet.

Miller had thought at first that maybe his pa wasn't sobering up enough to make his way home, and then maybe that he was off looking for ma. He even wondered for a time if pa had killed his ma or if he was dead himself. It was strange to think such things, but it didn't feel totally unnatural.

Miller raised the axe again and brought the bit down and split a chunk of maple. His thoughts went back to the dead men.

He raised the axe. It wasn't no good thinking about it. It made him feel ill and weak. That was the last thing he needed now.

He let his mind go blank and swung the axe again, and again. The jumbled pile of firewood grew.

It was late by the time the bus stopped down at the road and Jeannie got off and began walking up the dirt drive toward the house. Miller was sweating and wearing just his shirt, and the woodpile had grown. His mind was calmer.

Bailey got up and trotted out to walk with Jeannie. Miller watched her come near and he set the axe beside the chopping block, wiped his face, and said, "Your friend's pa was here."

Jeannie looked at him sideways. "Who?"

"Slocum."

She shook her head. "He's not really my friend."

Miller stretched his neck and rubbed a muscle to work out a kink. "I know he's not your friend. It was Rubylee's father."

"Oh, Rubylee."

"Who did you think I meant?"

Jeannie called over her shoulder from the bottom step. "Nobody."

"Wait a minute."

But she ran up the steps away from him. "No. I'm hungry. And I want to eat something that ain't made from peanut butter for once."

7

MILLER TURNED the TV on that night. It hadn't been used much since ma left. He adjusted the rabbit-ear antenna and sat on the couch while the news played, waiting for the story about the missing men.

They were two brothers. Everett and Dorsey Bowman. Their pictures came up on the screen. It was the men from the woods.

Jeannie came out of her room and sat beside Miller. They listened in silence and when it ended Jeannie asked, "What else did they say?"

Miller raised an eyebrow. "They were brothers. Gave their names."

Jeannie twisted her hands in her lap. "Brothers?"

"I guess so."

A reporter was asking anyone who knew or saw anything regarding the two men to call a number that was at the bottom of the screen. The reporter was standing in front of a house, and the camera panned up over the woman's shoulder, then a photo appeared in the corner of the frame showing the missing men together with some other people.

It was a quick image, but Miller saw Jeannie flinch. She looked at Miller. "Did you see that?"

"It won't matter. They won't find them. Or the truck."

"That was Casey Bowman."

"Who's Casey Bowman?"

"In the picture."

Miller blinked. "You knew those men? Why didn't you say so?"

"No. Not the men. Casey. He's in the junior high. I know him. We had to square dance together in gym class last year. He reminds me of it every time I see him."

Miller looked at his sister and thought about her square dancing with a boy he didn't know named Casey Bowman. He didn't like it, though he had no business thinking that way. "Why would they put his picture on?"

Jeannie sat up, twitched, sat back down. "The family picture they showed at the end." She pointed at the TV, but the picture she meant was gone.

Miller felt his chest compress.

Jeannie said, "That was Casey's pa in the woods."

No. They didn't know those men. They didn't want to know them.

"And his brother. That was Casey's pa and uncle."

Miller got up and turned the TV off. He turned to Jeannie. "This doesn't change anything. We still have to—"

Jeannie leaned into her lap and let out a long, keening howl. "Oh my god. You killed Casey's father."

Something that felt sticky like molasses moved into Miller's head. He tried to make it stop. "He was going to—"

Jeannie's howl became a shriek. "This is so wrong."

"What they were gonna do was wrong." He reached out a hand to Jeannie, but she slapped it away.

"Where is our pa?" Jeannie hissed. "Huh? Where is he? Tell me."

"We've talked about this. We just have to—"

"Maybe that's what happened to him. Somebody killed pa, and we'll never know about it. Just like Casey doesn't know."

Miller ran a hand over his jaw. He felt the sting of the cut on his lip and the ache of the bruises where the knuckles had struck. The dead man's knuckles. Casey Bowman's father, Everett. He was the one who'd come after Jeannie, who Miller had slashed with the shovel. Miller forced his thoughts upward. "We don't know if pa is dead."

"But you've thought about it."

"Thinking about it doesn't help us."

Jeannie hiccupped back another squeal. "Casey's pa is dead and he don't even know it."

"You said that."

"I danced with him."

He knew.

"And he'll never know what happened to his pa."

"If we're lucky."

The squeal came out full force now. "Don't that make you feel bad?"

"Of course it does."

"Makes you feel what we done was wrong."

Miller breathed. "Of course what we did was wrong. But there weren't no other way."

A wet bubble sputtered from Jeannie's throat.

Miller reached a hand out and let it touch softly on Jeannie's arm. She let him.

Her head bobbed once and she wiped her eyes. "It ain't right."

"I know it."

A few more stifled sobs bubbled from Jeannie. Then she fought them down.

Miller watched. There was nothing more he knew to say.

Jeannie gathered herself and leaned forward. Miller's hand slipped away. Jeannie looked up at him. "Where's my mamma?" She rocked forward and back on the edge of the couch. "Why would she leave us?"

Miller searched for words, found his voice and said, "I don't know." It didn't sound like enough to say.

"Why?"

Miller shook his head.

"I can see daddy runnin' off for a spell, but why would mamma leave us? What would make her do that?"

"We can't…"

"It was pa made her leave."

Miller guessed that was probably it, but there were worse things that might've happened to his ma that had run through his head. He kept those thoughts there.

Jeannie looked up. "What worries me most about pa is that his truck is still here."

Miller sighed. "I've been wondering how long until one of us said it."

"He'd come back for it."

Miller had prepared his answer. He'd readied it to give some hope to Jeannie, and to himself. "Unless he got into something good. Maybe he got himself a new truck."

Jeannie looked at him sideways. "You think?"

"Could be."

"That don't sound like what would happen to pa."

"We can hope."

She didn't look convinced. Jeannie's eyes roamed the room, over the empty chair where ma would have sat, the mat by the door where pa's boots would have been. "What is happening to us?" Her voice bobbled and broke, and a hand trembled up to wipe an eye.

Miller's mouth opened. He closed it. There were no words he could find.

They stayed like that for a time, Jeannie restless and reaching for her eyes. Then Jeannie's body stilled and she sat back on the couch.

Finally, Miller said, "You better now?"

"No."

A silence walked slowly between them. Jeannie stood and pulled the throw from the back of the couch around her shoulders. "Is there anything else you want to know?"

"No."

She turned toward her room.

Miller let her take a few steps, then called, "Yes."

Jeannie stopped and looked over her shoulder. "Yes what?"

"Yes there's something else I want to know."

"What is it?"

"Have you fed Bailey?"

"Of course I fed Bailey. He'd be all up on you if I hadn't. Why would I forget to feed him?"

Miller grinned. "Because you're a doofus."

Jeannie's face darkened. "Not the right time," she said, and stomped to her room and slammed the door.

Miller stood alone and listened to the wind on the windowpanes and the tick of wood burning in the potbelly stove.

8

MILLER WOKE in the night. A swath of moonlight cut through the window by his bed and laid a path to the door.

The sound that had woke him thudded again. Footsteps at his door, and then Jeannie was standing in the moonlight looking at him. "You awake?"

He rolled his head toward her. "Yeah."

"I'm cold. I can't sleep."

"Get another blanket."

"I did."

Miller pushed up on an elbow and squinted at his sister. Her shoulders were hunched and she held a blanket wrapped tightly around them. "You all right?"

"I can't sleep."

He lowered himself back down into the bed. "Take Bailey."

"I can't. He wants to be with you."

Miller felt the lump at the bottom of his bed. When he poked Bailey with a foot, the dog adjusted his position and remained on the bed. "Want me to get up and put some wood in the stove?"

Jeannie stepped through the moonlight into Miller's room and stood beside his bed. "We could sleep together. Like when we were kids."

Miller hesitated.

Jeannie's shoulders bunched under the blanket.

"We're not kids anymore," Miller said.

"I know. I can't sleep."

"OK." Miller scooted back in the bed and pulled the edge of the covers over for her.

Jeannie slipped the blanket from her shoulders and draped it over the bed, then moved in beside him. Bailey whined softly and moved into the space left for him at their feet.

Miller felt the cold coming from Jeannie's body. He kept some space between them and waited for her to settle and for the heat from him to help warm her.

After a few minutes, Jeannie's breathing slowed and she stopped shivering. When Miller thought she was asleep, she whispered to him, "Are we gonna be OK?"

Miller didn't know, but he said, "We have to be."

He waited again, and again Jeannie's breathing grew quiet and he thought she was asleep. Instead, she said, "I worry about…"

A long moment passed when he thought they might both fall asleep.

Then Jeannie finished it. "Too many things."

Miller sighed. "Everybody does. The older you get. You grow up, there are things to worry about. If you don't worry a little, you're doing something wrong. You're not growing up."

"So it's OK?"

"A little. You can't let the worrying get to you. You have to be able to let it go."

Some time passed. Jeannie said, "Like mamma?"

"Ma?"

"Mamma worried about things."

"She did. Ma worried about us. About taking care of us."

Jeannie sniffed. "Is that why she left? It was too much for her? The worrying?"

Miller let his arm drift onto his sister's shoulder. "No. That's not why she left. She loves us."

Miller might have heard another sniff from Jeannie. He said, "Things were complicated with ma and pa. She didn't leave because of us." He moved his hand gently on Jeannie's shoulder. "OK?"

She didn't answer, but her shoulder softened.

"Are you cold right now?"

"No."

"You feel OK right now?"

"I guess."

"Safe enough for now?"

She settled farther down into the bed. "Yeah."

"Then go to sleep."

9

MILLER STIRRED. Jeannie was back in her own bed sleeping. Bailey was curled at her feet.

He closed her bedroom door and went to the kitchen and stuffed paper and tinder into the potbelly, stacked two pieces of good hardwood on top, and lit the tinder. He watched the flame lick upwards for a minute before he closed the stove door and let the heat build up.

When Jeannie got up, he cooked eggs and made toast and coffee. While he worked, Jeannie sat at the table and picked at dirt under her fingernails. When she saw Miller watching her, she got up and poured herself a half cup of coffee and looked in the refrigerator. "No cream?"

Miller turned an egg. "No. Not milk neither."

Jeannie opened the sugar jar and spooned some into her cup. "We should get some."

Miller was drinking a cup black. "That'd be nice." He pointed with the spatula at a cupboard door. "Get out some plates?"

She did, and Miller loaded them with eggs and toast.

They sat to eat, and Jeannie said, "Potatoes'd be nice too."

Miller forked eggs onto a piece of toast. "We got potatoes. I didn't cook any. At least it's not peanut butter."

Bailey came to their feet to beg for scraps, and when they didn't offer any he laid by the potbelly and looked content enough.

When they had nearly finished eating, Jeannie announced flatly, "I ain't going to school today."

Miller didn't even look up. "Me neither."

They finished eating and picked up the dishes and Miller washed. He was letting the dish water out and Jeannie was wiping the plates dry when she said, "Was I…"

He left it hang. Squeezed the dishrag and spread it on the edge of the sink.

"Was it weird last night?"

"Was what weird?"

She cut a hard sideways glance at him.

"No, it wasn't too weird."

"Because we haven't…done that for a long time."

"Done what?"

She rolled her shoulders. "Sleeping."

"We sleep every night."

She gave him the hard look again.

Miller waited, then decided to say it. "Doofus."

She snapped the dish towel at him. "Simpleton."

He slapped the towel away. "Can't even get the dog to sleep with you."

Jeannie squeaked. "Bailey's a boy. I don't stink bad enough for him to sleep with me."

Bailey looked at them with lazy eyes. Miller grinned. "You stink bad enough on your own."

She snapped the towel again, but he slipped out of range, grabbed his coat, and went out to the front porch.

She followed him out a few minutes later, holding a blanket around her shoulders. The morning was quiet and cold. Miller watched Jeannie's breath come out in clouds. The school bus had already gone by, and the Jacksons' truck next door was gone. Birds sounded in the hills behind them.

Jeannie leaned against the porch rail. "What are you gonna do today?"

Miller hunched his shoulders. "Don't know. Cut wood, I guess."

"We need some."

"Gonna need a lot."

"We could have some dropped off," Jeannie said. "Lots of folks around here cut wood and would bring it right to the house."

"Sure enough. But wood costs money, and we don't have a lot."

Her eyes roamed over the hills and trees and fallen leaves. "How much?"

He thought about his answer for a long time, then said, "Enough for now. But we're going to have to figure something out."

A crow cawed, then another. Then the birds were making a racket, puncturing the quiet of the morning.

"You got some ideas?"

He did. "It'll be all right," he said. "I got some ideas." He pulled work gloves from his pocket and put them on. "But for now, I'm gonna cut wood."

Jeannie straightened from the railing. "I can help."

"You can." Miller turned toward the woodpile, and Jeannie went in the house to get into work clothes.

They worked for a while in the sunlight. Miller split wood on the block and stacked it. Jeannie dragged pieces to the sawbuck, and Miller helped her lift them into the trough and let Jeannie cut them to length with the chainsaw.

She was good with the saw. Miller had been cutting with it at her age, but he hadn't expected his sister to take to it like she had. Jeannie knew how to field-sharpen the blade with the rat-tail rasp and file the depth gauges. She was careful about greasing the bar and setting the tension on the chain, and she placed her feet well and kept the saw at a good angle in case it might bind and buck.

Jeannie was strong and braced herself to use her strength for the bottom cut, then laid the blade on top and let the saw do the work on the way down. And she was economical with fuel, which Miller appreciated almost as much as how well she cut wood.

They worked for a time longer. When they needed to mix more fuel for the saw and Miller was ready for a break from splitting, they stopped and sat on the woodpile. Miller took off his gloves. "It feels good to be distracted."

Jeannie grimaced. "Now that you've mentioned it, we're not so distracted anymore."

He wiped his brow. "I guess that's right."

The hills grew quiet now that the sawing and chopping had stopped. Jeannie said, "We should check on them."

Miller looked sideways at her. "Who?"

"Those men."

"I hope you're not saying what I think you're saying."

"We need to make sure, you know. They're like you said."

"They are."

"I know. I mean, I know they're…"

"They're dead."

"I seen that. But I didn't see, you know…"

Miller did know. And he knew this wasn't going anywhere good. "But you didn't see what I done with them."

"No."

"It's better that you don't know."

"We just have to make sure no one will find them. We should go check."

Miller rubbed his eyes and blew out a breath. "Jeannie–"

"I know."

"You don't know. Going back there is the worst thing we could do. We need to stay away."

Jeannie's head hung over and she looked at her toes.

Miller thought about it before he said it. "You're not still thinking about Casey Bowman not knowing what happened to his pa?"

"No." She dug at the edge of a fingernail, seemed to realize what she was doing, and stopped. "I was. But now I'm just scared someone will find them."

"You know they won't. I took care of that."

"It's just, you seen 'em. I keep imagining…things. If I could see them, maybe I'd be sure."

Miller stood and went over to Jeannie and laid a hand on her shoulder. "You have to stop. You don't want to see them. You can't, anyway."

Jeannie's shoulders bobbed.

"It's best we just forget about them. We'll get back to work cutting and I won't bring it up again."

Miller went to the block and set a chunk of fresh-cut wood on top. Jeannie stayed where she was and didn't get up to help.

Miller chopped.

After a time, Jeannie got up and drank from the water bottle they'd brought out, then picked up the saw and inspected the blade. When she was happy with it, she pulled the cord and the engine flared and she began to cut.

When they had been hungry for a while and it was close enough to lunch time anyway, they used the barrow to carry the wood they had cut and split to the lean-to and stack it. They'd added a good bit to the pile. Miller squinted at the length of wood to try and see it in day-sized chunks. He counted the measures down to when they would run out. It wouldn't be long.

"What's to eat?" Jeannie said as Miller was tipping the barrow up against the pile.

"Leftover chili."

"Crackers?"

Miller shook his head. "There ain't no crackers."

"We should get some. There's still a mess of chili. It's better with crackers."

Jeannie didn't know he'd been taking food from the charity barrel. There was a little bit of money. Enough they could buy crackers. Put a little gas in the truck. But without knowing when ma or pa would come back, if they ever would, Miller was slow to spend much. He'd seen his ma pinch pennies when pa wasn't inclined to work, but pa always eventually brought in some money when he had to. Now they didn't have that anymore, and he wanted to spend for crackers but it made him second-guess himself.

Finally, Miller said, "I suppose crackers or something would be good."

When they were inside and Miller was warming the chili on the stove, Jeannie said, "Can I use your phone?"

"What for?"

"I want to call Rubylee."

"You know they can't answer during school."

"I know. I'll leave her a message."

Miller looked in the cupboard for bread. There were a couple of stale heels slid behind the tub of peanut butter. He dribbled oil onto the heels and placed them into the iron pan to warm and soften. "Can't it wait?"

"I want to make sure she waits for me after school. I'm going over there and I don't want her to leave before I get there."

"You didn't ever seem to need to call Rubylee before when you went over there."

Jeannie got a sour look on her face, and Miller pulled the phone from his pocket and looked at it. "There's not many minutes left. I only got a few dollars on it."

Jeannie reached for the phone, but he hadn't offered it yet and it stayed in his palm. She said, "If you got a real phone you wouldn't have to worry about running out of minutes."

"Look," he said. "We've talked about this. We don't have a lot of money to spend on phones. Just for what we need."

Jeannie's frown grew deeper. "What do you need a phone for anyway? You never use it."

Miller pointed a finger at her. "Ma or pa might call. They might try to reach us and I need to have time on it so I can answer."

"Ha. Ma or pa ain't never used a cell phone in their life. They probably don't even know the number for yours."

Heat rose in Miller's cheeks. "They got the number. They can use if they…"

"If they what? They don't have your number. You told it to them and they forgot. They don't have phones to put your number into."

Miller slapped the phone down on the table. "Here's the stupid phone. I don't know what's so damn important about calling Rubylee. You're going to see her later anyway."

Jeannie snatched up the phone and said, "What did Rubylee's pa talk to you about when he was over here?"

"I told you. He was just checking in."

"Why would he do that? Ain't nobody ever come over here to check on us before."

Miller's mind went to the food barrel again, still wondering if Mrs. Slocum had seen him taking things from it. If she'd seen him steal the cupcakes. "Things aren't like they were before," he said. "People might be starting to wonder, what with nobody seeing ma or pa around for a while."

"So he didn't say anything?"

"He saw we were all right, and he left." Miller did not tell Jeannie that he had shown Mr. Slocum the bruises on his face to make him think that their pa had done it.

Jeannie took the phone to her room. Miller regretted giving it to her. She'd use up what minutes were left.

Miller called for his sister a few minutes later when the chili was hot. The toasted bread was good with it, and Miller had a cup of coffee left over from breakfast. After they ate, Jeannie cleaned up the dishes and put the big pot of leftover chili back into the fridge.

Miller went out to the porch to survey the woodpile again. He'd taken the phone back, and he pulled it from his pocket and looked at the calls. Jeannie had called two different numbers. He checked the balance and told himself he'd have to think about putting more money on it.

He looked at the phone for a long time, but he didn't dial back the numbers to see who Jeannie had made the calls to.

10

MILLER PULLED his gloves on. They were slow to start work again after lunch. There wasn't much wood left to cut and split. Miller started in on that, and Jeannie went for a walk in the woods with Bailey.

When he was finished with the wood, Miller went in and laid down for a minute on the couch. He woke when Jeannie came in. "Can I use the truck to go over to Rubylee's?"

"What?" He sat up and rubbed the back of his neck.

"I want to go to Rubylee's."

"OK. But you don't need to take the truck."

"I've done it before."

"Driving the truck through the woods is one thing. Going in traffic is another."

"I drove home the other night. Then back to get you."

"That was different."

"You've let me drive to the store."

"Once. In the dark. When no one could see, and I was with you."

Jeannie cocked a hip. "I've driven to Rubylee's."

Miller got up from the couch and his eyes went to the kitchen door and the hook next to it where they kept the keys. She could have, and he wouldn't have known.

He rubbed the back of his neck some more. "We need to get more firewood anyway."

"We got enough for now."

"There's never enough. Pa taught us that."

"We got as much wood as pa ever had cut."

The stiff spot in his neck would not let go of him. "We don't want to do exactly like pa did."

"But we have to do like pa said? Not what he done?"

"Look, we're just gonna need more wood to burn. We may as well get more now while we've been working at it."

Jeannie's eyes bore at Miller. He went to the kitchen to get some distance from her. "What are you in such a hurry for? You can walk."

Jeannie spun and went into her room and slammed the door. Through it, she shouted, "I helped you cut wood all morning."

Miller slipped the truck key from the hook and buried it deep in his pocket. He went to Jeannie's door and stood outside it and said, "If we get caught now, they'll haul us off. We have to be careful."

There was a moment of quiet, then Jeannie's voice came back. "I won't get caught. I'm a good driver. You said that."

"I know. You drive as well as most folks, I guess. But if someone sees you."

The door was quiet. Miller walked away and paced the kitchen floor a couple of times.

He came back to Jeannie's door and said, "I know it's been hard." He waited, but there was no reply. "I could drop you off."

The door creaked open. "Give me a few minutes." And the door creaked closed again.

Miller waited and it was more than a few minutes. When Jeannie came out, she was dressed in a clean pair of jeans and a fresh shirt. Miller considered her. "You did something to your hair." It was brushed back, and there was a clip in one side.

"There's nothing wrong with not looking like a hillbilly sometimes. You ought to try it."

Miller ignored her and turned away. "I'll be in the truck."

She was on his heels and they climbed into the truck together and they went the whole ride without saying much, Jeannie working the radio to try to bring in a song she liked.

When Miller stopped in the Slocum's dirt drive he said, "What time you want me to come get you?"

"I can walk back."

He tightened his grip on the steering wheel. "All that trouble about getting a ride over here, and now you'll just walk home?"

"I can probably get a ride." She smiled. "It'll save gas anyway."

"If you come back after dark you're gonna need one. Call me if you need to."

Jeannie stepped out of the truck without answering and walked up to the house.

Miller didn't understand girls and didn't know why he'd gotten one for a sister when he felt so unprepared for it. He turned the truck around, and on the way home he turned into Johnson's Market to get crackers and hamburger and macaroni and a couple of other things he thought Jeannie would like. He paid cash for everything and never once even looked in the food barrel.

When he pulled off the road onto the drive that went up and branched to the left for their house and to the right for the Jacksons, there was a truck at the split. Slocum again, he thought, but the color of the truck was different and it was older and more beat-up than Slocum's truck. He could see the Jacksons' light was on and the visitors might have been there for them, but it was an odd place to park and he didn't like it.

He drove past slow and looked over. Two men were sitting in the truck and the cab was hazy from cigarette smoke. Miller pulled forward to the house and turned the truck around next to the porch so it faced the road. Then he went inside and locked the door and went to the closet where they kept the shotgun.

He did not put the truck key back on the hook by the door.

11

MILLER WATCHED through the window as the men left their truck at the split in the drive and walked up to the house. These men were not with the sheriff's. They did not look like county workers, and they were not with Child Services. Those people Miller would talk to. He would tell them that everything was all right and they were fine. He would convince them to go away.

But these men were not what he was prepared for. These looked like the kind of men his pa ran with. Worn and dirty jackets, stringy hair and stringier beards. Shoulders cocked and a look on their faces that said they'd seen trouble and they weren't afraid of it.

The men's jaws were set and they hunched forward as they climbed the porch steps. When the knock came on the door it was too loud. "We come to see Zebulon."

Miller opened the door and backed them up with the shotgun. One of the men raised his hands and said, "Whoa, boy. Put that thing down."

The other pulled his jacket back and put a hand to his belt. Miller trained the gun on the one reaching. "You got something in there, mister, you keep it where it is."

The man with his hands up was thin and had a beard that wouldn't grow in right on one side of his face. Miller guessed it was from scars underneath. But he focused instead on the other man with the handle of a pistol showing at his hip.

The man didn't want to move his hand away from the pistol. Miller took a half-step forward with the shotgun and the man's hand moved up and away from the butt of his gun. "Shit, boy. Why you greet us that way? We're here to see Zebulon. That your pappy?"

Miller's eyes flicked between the men, then back to the one with the pistol. "No one calls my pa Zebulon."

It was true. Pa had always gone by Zeb. He liked to say it was one way he could tell the ones who were there to see him from the ones who were there to get him. If they said Zebulon, run.

The men's hands were still up, and a look passed between them. The one Miller had the shotgun aimed at said, "Then what do they call him? We sure as shit know him as Zebulon." His hands dropped a little. "Put that thing away. Where'd you learn to point a gun at folks come to pay a visit?"

"I'll keep it," Miller said.

"Boy, you're overreacting."

Miller took a breath. "Why you got a gun in your belt?"

The man grinned. "Case someone overreacts."

Miller eased back a step toward the door. "My pa ain't here."

Both of the men's hands went down to their belts. "Where is he?"

"He's workin' at a sawmill over outside of Munson."

The men exchanged looks again. Now the second man spoke. "That don't sound like Zebulon."

Miller let it hang.

"When's he comin' home?"

"He ain't been home for a while. He's sleeping over there sometimes. Lot of work."

The man shook his head. "No sir, that don't sound like him at all."

The man with the pistol said, "I ain't never heard of no sawmill over by Munson."

"Got them an old Cadillac engine hooked up to a big saw blade. Runnin' it out under a pole barn. I been down there and seen it."

Miller didn't know where the lie came from. It flowed from him like taffy, sticky on his tongue and hard to swallow. He didn't know how long the lie would hold, and his mind was already spinning out new lies to pile on the first if he needed them.

The man with the gun said, "Munson. That's a long way."

Miller gave them some time to think about it, then said, "It's where the work is."

He could see the men growing more confident. They stepped farther apart and the man with the pistol said, "Now that just don't sound quite right."

"You doubt my word?"

"Now don't get your panties in a bunch," the man said. He cocked a hip forward. Miller kept the barrels on him.

"Your mamma home? Maybe we can talk some sense to her."

Miller didn't like the men spreading away from each other. If he backed up any farther to keep them both in line with the shotgun, he'd have to step back into the house. He didn't like that either. "Ma ain't keen for company."

The man leaned forward. "Listen, boy. We ain't here askin' to see Zebulon. We're here telling you we're going to see him. You best get that in your head and things'll go more smooth for you."

Miller said nothing. He let the men look at him for a long time.

"Well? What you got to say, boy? This is serious. You heared about them men what didn't come home the other night? You know about that?" The man moved forward now, pulled his jacket around to the side so he'd have a clean reach for the handle of the pistol in his belt. "Them men's because of your daddy. He done that. Now put that thing down before I have to take it from you and teach you a lesson your daddy should'a done a long time ago."

Miller knew what his pa would do if men came to the house and spoke to him like this. And he knew that one day he'd have to be the man of his own house and decide how he would deal with men like this. That day felt like it had come early for him.

Miller stepped back to open some space to move the barrels of the shotgun between the two men. He was at the door stoop now, nowhere further back to go except into the house. He wasn't going to do that. "You're not the first man to show me he's packin' powder in his pants. You reach for that gun and I'll take your hand off and half your gut before you can thank your maker he put you here."

The man's eyes narrowed on Miller and his face grew dark. Miller knew he was thinking about it.

"Your business is with my pa," Miller said. "He ain't here. I am, and I'm telling you to git."

The second man had backed away, but the man with the pistol stood with a hand out at his side like a movie gunslinger.

Miller's finger trembled on the trigger, but he kept himself squared. "I ain't afraid to test the law. I'm here at my own house, telling you to leave. You ain't done that. I'm standing my ground. The law is on my side." He flicked his eyes toward the neighbors' house through the trees. "The Jacksons are home. You see their truck? They'll hear the blast and come over. One of you might make it to plead your case. But maybe neither of you."

The man wiggled his fingers toward the butt of his gun. "You're making a mistake, boy."

Miller kept his eyes level with the man's. "I'll make it."

Anger roiled off the man, but he let his jacket fall back over the pistol and turned away. He stopped at the bottom of the steps and hissed at Miller, "I ever get the chance, boy, and I'm gonna pull your gizzard out through your throat."

The man joined the other and they started for their truck.

Miller followed behind them.

The angry one spat, "You put that thing away now. We're leaving."

Miller kept step with them and kept the gun up. "No sir. I'll walk you down."

The man twisted his head over his shoulder but continued walking away. "Motherfucker! Put it down."

Miller kept his eyes up and the barrel of the gun level. Weeds slapped his pant legs as he walked. "When I see your rear bumper disappearing down that road."

The man kicked dirt and spat. "You're making a mistake."

Miller kept coming after them. "Probably so."

12

MILLER LEFT the shells in the shotgun and propped it against the wall beside the door. It was breaking a rule, leaving the gun out and loaded, but these weren't normal times.

He locked the doors and sank into the easy chair in the living room. The house was quiet and he was alone. Even Bailey was off somewhere like he did, chasing something or looking for more to eat than what they had given him.

Miller felt as if he was descending on a dark trajectory that hillfolk around here had fallen prey to for generations. He was taking Jeannie with him, and they were accelerating as they fell. Miller could not see the end of the fall.

His regrets came and perched on his shoulder and spoke to him like tiny birds. They told him that those men would come back, and things would go harder the next time. Jeannie might not be safe. He'd been trying to be a man among men he didn't want to become like. But that's not how things seemed to go most often in these hills. Men became men like those that had come before them. He

couldn't see the end of that road either. There had to be a
smarter way.

Miller tried to quiet his mind and let the demons in his
head finish their lecture so he could let them go and forget
them. He eventually closed his eyes, and when he woke he
wondered what it meant that the men had said his pa caused
the disappearances of Everett and Dorsey Bowman. Did it
mean they thought his pa was alive, and that he'd done it?

He couldn't square it in his thinking. He'd been consid-
ering that his pa was dead, that the men he'd been bootleg-
ging with had done him in. Now he would have to go look
for his pa, and he didn't like that either. Better to starve here
alone than to get mixed up with those people again.

Miller fought it, but his mind closed in on those
thoughts and held him. Eventually he drifted off to sleep
again. When he woke it was dark and the house was cold.

He rose and put wood in the potbelly and lit the fire.
Bailey had come in and was laying by his bowl looking for
food.

Miller looked through the house for Jeannie, called for
her out in the yard. Was he supposed to have gone to get her?

He took the phone from his pocket and checked it.
There were no missed calls.

His finger went to the first number Jeannie had called
earlier that day and he pressed the button. A greeting message told him, "This is Dundee. Y'all leave a message if you
want to."

He hung up. Dundee was Rubylee Slocum's brother. It
seemed odd, but that was probably Jeannie trying to find
Rubylee.

He called the second number. A girl's voice said, "Jeannie?"

Miller said, "No, this is Miller Brenning. I'm looking for Jeannie."

"Oh. She was here."

"Rubylee?"

"Yeah."

"Is Jeannie there now?"

"No. Her and Dundee went out."

"Out?"

"Those two been carryin' on."

"Carrying on?"

"He took her in the Chevy."

"Took her? Where?"

There was a pause. "Datin', I guess. I think that's what they've been doing."

His thoughts swam. "How long has this been going on?"

"No that long. It's a new thing."

Like it was nothing. "You're OK with that?"

"I don't know. It's weird because Dundee is my brother. But if Jeannie's got to have someone to lean on, I guess she could do worse."

"Lean on?"

There was a long pause. "I guess it started after your mother…"

Neither of them finished it.

Rubylee said, "I don't think it's serious. Jeannie's just looking for a…"

"A distraction?"

"I guess that's what it is."

Questions crawled through Miller's head. So where does Dundee take her? What do they do? Instead he said, "When will they be back?"

"Oh, I don't know. Dundee'll probably take her home I guess."

Miller said thanks and pressed the button to disconnect. The demons on his shoulder were speaking again. Jeannie was growing up. That was the natural course of things. But there was a pace to this, and there wasn't ma with them to show Jeannie the proper way of things.

And Jeannie was too young. Dundee was too old for her. Dundee could drive and take her places where they could be alone. He didn't want to, but he'd have to talk to Dundee.

He might have to do more than that.

Miller tried to press the dark thoughts from his mind. It was too easy to get started down that path.

13

MILLER SAT in the dark and second-guessed himself. His pa made things bad by assuming the worst, believing the least in others, getting angry regardless of the truth. Miller didn't have to be like that. Jeannie could be acting right with Dundee. Dundee could be acting right with Jeannie. He might make things worse by going about talking to Jeannie the wrong way. Or Dundee. It would be easy to take a misstep.

Miller wondered how he might be different if his pa had trusted him more. If he'd had someone else to show him to do things right with other people.

He was still sitting when headlights swung up the drive and approached the house. A vehicle door opened and closed, and the headlights turned and swung away.

A moment later Jeannie came in and turned on the lights and looked at him. "Why were you sitting in the dark?"

Miller moved his head around slowly. "Tired."

"Uh huh. She hung her coat on one of the pegs by the door. "Why's the shotgun out?"

"Some men were here."

Jeannie froze. "Men? What did they want?"

"They were looking for pa."

She came and sat on the couch across from him and twisted her hands. "Daddy."

"Yeah."

"Why were they looking for daddy?"

Miller let the words out without trying to stop them. "They said it was pa's fault those men didn't come home."

Jeannie's hands twisted faster. She tried to settle them on her lap. "The men who..."

He nodded. "The Bowmans."

"But we... They can't..."

"Uh huh. Why would they think it was pa?"

Jeannie shivered. "I don't like this."

"Me neither. But it means they think pa is still alive. Or seem to."

Jeannie breathed. "OK."

"They called him Zebulon."

"No one calls daddy Zebulon."

"That's right."

Jeannie straightened her back. "Except them bootleggers."

"That's the way I figured it."

Miller let it sink in with Jeannie. Finally she said, "Them is the nastiest people pa ever brung over here. The nastiest people I ever met."

"I know it. Whoever was here today was plenty nasty."

Jeannie's eyes went to the shotgun by the door. "You think it was them?"

"I don't know for sure."

Jeannie cut her eyes back to Miller. "You run them off?"

"Barely."

Her shoulders began to sway. "I don't like this."

"I've got to find them. Before they can come back here again looking for pa."

"Jesus, Miller, you can't do that. You can't go *looking* for them."

"We can't wait for them to come back."

Jeannie got up and paced awkwardly in the small space between them. "We need to know what's going on."

"We need to find pa."

Jeannie stopped her steps. "You really think he's alive?"

"Them men seem to."

She worried her hands some more.

Miller sighed and rubbed his forehead hard. He got up. "Dundee give you a ride home?"

"I said he would."

"OK. I didn't remember." He tried out what he'd been thinking, see if Jeannie would take it okay. "Did you go over there to see him, or Rubylee?"

"Dundee just gave me a ride home. God, why you gotta make something of it?"

Miller stumbled on. "It's just that you're growing up."

Jeannie's hands fluttered to her hips. "What does that mean? Ain't I allowed to grow up?"

Slow it down, Miller thought. Easy. "Boys are going to start noticing you, is all."

She started toward her room, but Miller held a hand up and she stopped. He said, "You know what those men in the woods had their minds on. What did ma tell you about it?"

"About what?"

"Boys."

"She didn't say much."

"Did she tell you not to be alone with them? Including in cars?"

Jeannie's face blossomed red. "Dundee just gave me a ride. I told you that."

"Dundee is older than you."

"I've known him my whole life. Dundee is just being nice."

"OK."

"I told you—"

"OK. I believe you."

Jeannie glowered. "You ain't ma. Why are you treating me like this?"

"Because there ain't no ma now."

Jeannie spun away.

"There's supper," he called after her.

She went in her room and slammed the door, and called through it, "I'm not hungry."

He warmed some chili in a pan on the stove and set it on the table with two bowls. Then Miller called across the empty house, "There's crackers. And more of those cupcakes you like."

There was no answer. He ate some chili.

Bailey laid beside the potbelly and begged, but Miller did not give him any of the chili or put food in his bowl. That was Jeannie's job.

He ran water and cleaned his bowl and called out to Jeannie again. "It'll be here if you want it."

Nothing.

He put wood into the potbelly. "I put a log in the stove for you. Bailey's hungry."

Nothing.

He put on his coat and reached in his pocket for the truck key. "I'm leaving for a while."

Jeannie's door opened and her head came out. "You're leaving?"

"Yeah."

She emerged a little more from her room. "Where are you going?"

"I told you."

"You never told me."

"Look for pa. If he's alive."

"You'll leave me here?"

"I don't want to. I have to. Lock the doors. If you need to, sneak out back and hide in the woods."

"Like we used to when daddy got…bad?"

Miller nodded. "Like that." He thought about it some more. "Maybe it'd be better you go back to Rubylee's."

"I can do it."

"Do what?"

"Hide. If I need to."

Miller knew she could. "Put Bailey out. He'll let you know if anyone comes."

"I wish I had a phone, to call if anything happened."

"There's only the one. You can't call me if you have it and I don't have one."

"I could call someone else."

"Who?" But he already knew.

"I could call Rubylee. Or Dundee."

Miller pulled the phone from his pocket and held it out for her. "Don't use it unless you need to. Not just for talking. There's not many minutes left."

Jeannie took the phone. "I know."

"Worst happens, there's the shotgun."

She shivered. "I could go with you."

"We both know you can't."

Jeannie's eye went down. "Where you gonna go?"

"Down to those places pa was selling shine to. Maybe somebody's seen him. Or knows something."

"Nobody'll tell you anything."

"They won't if I sit here and do nothing."

"What if you find those men who was here?"

Miller reached for his jacket on the peg. "I ain't figured that out yet, but at least we'll know where they are."

"I don't see how that will help a whole lot."

He turned for the door. "I ain't figured that out yet either."

14

MILLER KNEW these twisted backroads as if he'd been born with the map in his head. They were a part of his psyche that stretched back beyond his memory. He drove them now in the dark with reckless regard for the zags and turns that dropped sharply into gullies and ditches and waterways and trees.

He hoped where he was going someone would recognize him. Not the men who had come to the house, but someone who'd seen him before, with his pa.

His pa used to take him to the bars in the flatlands down along the river when he was in grade school.

Pa took Miller along sometimes for company, Miller guessed. Or just because that's what pa did. He never did explain himself much.

Miller didn't understand it in the beginning, but he knew his pa had something going on with the men at the bars. They would talk in hushed voices while Miller stood on a crate to play the pinball machines with coins his pa gave him. Sometimes his pa would go in the back with one of the men and he'd be gone a long time and maybe a woman would come out from behind the bar and pat Miller's head and say *Aren't you such a handsome little feller?* and ask him if he wanted a coke or a bag of chips.

Miller liked the women at the bars who doted on him, and he liked the games and the cokes and the snacks. And it didn't take him long to catch on to what his pa was doing.

Pa sold moonshine. He had a still somewhere up in the hills behind his cousin Rebel's place. Pa ran the still when he felt like it, which meant when he wanted money or owed someone. He refilled empty whiskey bottles, disguising the shine as real bottled whiskey.

Pa got proud of the way he was cheating the stupid folk who drank his shine and thought they were getting the real thing. He made sure to show Miller how smart his daddy was, took him in the back where the men who ran the bars tasted the shine. He sometimes gave Miller a tiny splash from a bottle and made him drink it. It always tasted awful. Then pa mixed a tiny splash with a splash of coke, and it still tasted bad.

"See?" pa had said, clapping his hands. "No difference. They think they're drinking Southern Comfort."

Miller tried to pretend he was proud of his pa, but he always drank long from the coke can to wash down the evil taste.

Pa's secret was flavoring the shine with wood chips he seared with a soldering torch. Drop the chips in the batch with a little sugar and let it soak, and pa said it made a hooch good enough for common folk who never drank anything from higher than the bottom shelf and couldn't tell shine from bottled in bond.

For the most part, Miller could steer his way to the pinball machines and avoid the tastings in the back rooms. He didn't know why his father often brought him to the bars with him, and he didn't like the men in the back rooms.

Pa never could work steady at the still, like anything, but it seemed to keep him in beer and cigarettes and money to shoot pool late into the night. Miller figured his ma knew what pa was doing, but he never saw a bootleg bottle in the house, and ma never said a word about it.

But then one spring there'd been some kind of dispute about the shine. Men came to the house to settle the matter. But the men were mean, and pa and them got to yelling and shoving and one of them busted a chair and said he was gonna put a hole in pa's kidney. Ma grabbed Miller and Jeannie and hustled them out the back and told Miller to take Jeannie into the woods and hide until it was over.

Pa was madder'n a cat in a wet sack when it was over. He and ma picked up the house and took the broken chair out onto the porch, and then pa got real quiet for a while.

A few days later some of the places that were selling pa's shine got raided. They brought in the county deputies and some state cars, and the arrests had lingered in the news and in the local gossip for weeks.

It was one of the few times Miller could remember his mother standing up to pa. She wouldn't cook or speak to him until pa said he'd scuttled the still and that was the end of the moonshining.

Some of the places that had been raided closed down, and some of the men who'd run them went to jail.

For a long time after that Miller believed his pa wasn't making whiskey. But pa had always kept secrets. Mysterious shapes appeared beneath a tarp in the back of the truck. Pa disappeared for long stretches of time without any explanation. This past spring he and ma had been fighting more than ever before, pa meaner than he'd ever been.

Then ma disappeared without a word.

Miller turned the truck onto a back lane. The darkened, treacherous road worried Miller a lot less than where he was going. Some of the places where his pa had sold liquor had changed names or started back up. He had a few in mind he'd seen his pa's truck at over the last months. He hoped to find one of the women who'd given him chips and a coke when he was a kid. He didn't think too hard about what else he might find.

Rudy's Bar sat on a sparse stretch of holler where two lonely roads made a tee. His pa had called the place Snakeroot, but there was no sign announcing any kind of town.

A few houses were spaced out along the intersection of the roads. The weedy dirt lot in front of the bar was crowded with seven or eight cars and trucks. Miller eased into a spot by the road.

It was different than he remembered, but Miller knew the place. He'd always been here during the day with his pa, when the place was empty and bright. Now it looked small and crowded and dim. He made a beeline for an empty booth in the back.

A handful of stools at the bar were mostly taken. Both pool tables squeezed into the back had games going, and the few other booths were filled. A TV played silently behind the bar, and country tunes from the jukebox blanketed the room.

Eyes from a man working at the bar followed Miller when he came in, then ignored him. Miller hunched in his booth and looked around. When his eyes roamed over a woman standing at the jukebox, she caught him looking and cocked a hip in his direction.

Miller looked away.

His eyes went around the place again and when they came back to the woman she was coming toward him. She stopped at the end of Miller's bench and said, "Hi."

He thought she was thirty, maybe. He wasn't good at guessing the ages of women older than him. Her jeans were tight and she wore a tiny jacket that looked like it could have been leather and a sweater that hung so low in the front when she bent that he felt his face flush at what was there.

Miller had been on some dates and thought he knew what to do with girls his age. He'd never really been comfortable around girls, but he could get by. This woman was something new. She wasn't like the women who had patted him on the head when he was younger and offered him cokes.

He said, "Hi."

She braced an arm on the table and looked him over. "What happened to you?"

Miller's hand went to his lip. "Chunk of wood splintered off the chopping block."

Her gaze lingered on the bruises. "Must have jumped up and hit you four or five times."

Miller knew it was a joke but he didn't laugh. The woman smiled at him and he said, "I'm looking for someone."

"Maybe you found her." She winked and motioned for him to move over in the seat. He did, and she slid in beside him.

She took off her tiny jacket and laid it across her lap. Then she shook her hair down over her shoulders and ran her fingers through the thick brown strands like she was squeezing water from them.

"So…," she said and turned to Miller.

He waited.

She tilted her head.

Miller thought of his ma. This woman was younger, but she was a woman, not like the girls he knew from school. She wasn't wearing makeup that he could tell, but her skin looked smooth and bright. Not like ma. His thoughts were jumbled.

The woman took some time to rearrange her jacket carefully in her lap and Miller thought she probably wanted him to watch her do that. Then she looked at Miller and said, "You wanna buy me a drink?"

"Uhm."

"It's OK. My friends are right over there." She pointed to two women who appeared to be trying to look like they were watching some guys shoot pool. "I'm just being friendly."

She smiled at him and he reached into his pocket and fumbled for his wallet and fished out some bills.

She picked a five from his hand. "They call me Johnnycakes."

"Johnnycakes?"

"I used to like to eat them a lot when I was a girl. You can call me Johnny."

He touched the tip of his cap out of habit. "Miller."

Johnny leaned close to Miller and said, "You want something too?"

He put his head down and said, "Beer."

She held up her hand with all five fingers out, and when he didn't seem to get it she put her mouth close to Miller's neck and said, "That's five more."

He gave her another bill and immediately felt sick about it. Ten dollars would go a long way for him and Jeannie.

Then Johnny got up and went to the bar and for a moment Miller thought both her and his money was gone. But then she came back carrying a glass filled with what looked like what his father used to mix in the back rooms, and a Bud for him.

Johnny sat close to Miller and lifted her glass. "Cheers."

He raised his bottle and they both took a drink. Johnny smiled at him for a moment. When he didn't say anything, she said, "I don't think I've seen you in here before?"

Miller shook his head.

"We don't get a lot of new faces." She twisted and leaned around Miller to get a good look at him. Her sweater fell away from her chest and Miller's eyes went to the soft white flesh that was exposed. She followed his eyes and said, "How old are you?"

Miller took a drink and set his bottle back down. "I'm really just here looking for someone."

"You said that."

He touched his bottle again, twisted it around, but left it on the table. "I really didn't mean to…"

"You didn't do anything. I did."

Miller's hands floated to the bottle and back again. He didn't know where to put them.

Johnny watched him. "Who'd you say you were looking for?"

Miller straightened. "Zeb Brenning."

She shook her head.

"My pa."

Now Johnny looked at Miller for a long time. "Why're you lookin' for your pa?"

He shrugged. Why would anybody? "Because he's gone, ma'am."

Johnny flinched. "Look, you can't buy me a drink and then call me ma'am."

"Yes m—"

She sighed. "Oh, for god's sake. You got a picture of him?"

Miller's eyes said Who?

"Your father."

He wagged his head. "No."

"Well what's he look like?"

"Black hair. Real curly. Always wears a red-and-black flannel jacket. He used to come in here a lot, a long time ago. I thought maybe he'd been back."

Johnny tapped a painted fingernail against the table. "What kind of trouble are you in?"

"No trouble. I'm just lookin' for my pa."

Something sad passed across Johnny's face. Her finger stopped tapping. She said, "I haven't seen anybody like that.

I can't help you." She picked up her glass and drank. "I wish I could."

Miller sat in the booth and felt like he was trapped. Johnny looked at him like she was trying to make up her mind about something. Finally, she sighed and said, "Look, we're just gonna have the one drink together and that's it. But do you wanna dance?"

He didn't, but before Miller could answer she had him up and was leading him to the little space in front of the jukebox where they could stand up and turn and maybe not bump into anybody.

The jukebox was playing Simple Man, and Johnny stepped close to Miller and put her arms around him. He circled his own arms behind her back and she leaned her head into his shoulder.

Miller had danced with girls before, but not like this. They were the only ones dancing, and Miller felt the eyes on them. Johnny pulled on him in a sad way like a moth drawn to a light.

The song mercifully ended and Miller looked around the room but no one seemed to be staring at them.

Johnny let go of Miller and stepped back. "Look, I enjoyed the dance, but I think you and I are here for different things."

His brain tingled. He felt relieved, but there was something else that might have been disappointment teasing his mind.

Then Johnny squeezed Miller's shoulder and melted away back to their table where she picked up her tiny jacket and headed for the women's room.

15

MILLER FLINCHED when laughter burst from behind him at the pool tables. He looked over. Two men he guessed were about Johnny's age didn't try to hide that they were the ones who'd laughed, and it was aimed at Miller.

Miller pulled his hat down and went to the booth for his jacket. This whole thing was a mistake. He should have come during the day, like he'd done with his pa when he was young. When the bars would be empty and maybe he could find someone who would talk to him. All he'd done here tonight was waste money.

One of the men who'd laughed stepped behind Miller when he reached into the seat for his jacket. When Miller turned, the man had blocked his way. "Looks like you struck out with Johnny."

Miller said nothing.

The man waved the tip of his pool cue back and forth. "Don't worry about it. She ain't an easy chick to bag. 'Specially if you ain't man enough to keep yourself from getting beaten up."

Miller ignored the man's comments about the marks on his face and what he'd said about Johnny. He tried to step around the man, but the man shifted to block Miller's path. "Hold on a minute. You don't have to leave 'cause you got shot down."

"I don't want no trouble. I was just here looking for somebody."

The man leaned forward on his toes, the pool cue still waving in front of him. "Looking for somebody?"

Miller tried to get his arms into the jacket, but the man was too close for it.

"You find him?"

"No."

"Maybe I can help."

Miller looked at the man, and at his friend who'd come over and stood next to him. He stepped sideways to get by. "I doubt it."

The man stepped around Miller and blocked his path again. "Now that's not a very nice thing to say."

Miller stood with his jacket in his hand. "What do you want?"

"I want to know who you're looking for. And what the fuck you think you were doing with Johnny."

Someone from across the room shouted, "Dean, knock it off."

The man blocking Miller's way looked over but ignored the voice. He stuck his jaw close to Miller's face. "What are you doing here, boy?"

Miller stood his ground. "Leaving."

"Not yet, you ain't. Who'd you come here looking for?"

There were eyes on them now. The music was still loud and Miller wondered how much the others could hear. He looked the man in the eye and said, "I'm looking for Zeb Brenning."

Nothing happened. Nobody seemed to hear or care. The man they'd called Dean ran a hand over his chin. "Zeb, huh?"

"You know him?"

"Who is he to you?"

"He's my pa."

Dean laughed. "You're here looking for your pa?"

Miller stepped away.

Dean blocked his path again. "Tell you what. You come shoot a game of pool with me and I'll tell you what I know about your ol' pa."

Miller tried to read the man, but there was no reading except meanness. He dropped his head and followed Dean to the pool table.

Now Miller was the moth, and he was flying into the flame. He picked a cue from the rack. The man named Dean laid a five-dollar bill on the edge of the table.

Miller felt sick as he counted out ones and laid them beside the five.

The man lifted the triangle from a rack of balls. "You know nine-ball?"

Miller knew. His pa had made sure any son of Zeb Brenning knew how to shoot nine-ball. Miller rested his cue on the edge of the table and said, "Ball in hand?"

The man's eyes came up.

"Scratch if it don't touch the lowest numbered."

The man shifted his feet. "Break, smartass."

Miller broke the rack and the five dropped. He turned to the one in the corner and dropped it into the pocket. The cue ball rolled away and left a good angle on the two. Behind that, the nine lurked near the side pocket.

When he walked around for the shot, the man put a hand on Miller's arm. "Slow down, boy. We didn't bring you over here to win a game."

Miller knew the routine. He'd seen his pa do it. The game was the nice way for them to take his money. He could lay it down now on the table, or he could fight these men for it in the parking lot. Miller knew that they didn't know anything about his pa, and he couldn't see a good way for this to end.

He dropped the two into the side and lined up on the three.

The man's friend stood from his stool and crossed his arms over his chest.

Miller dropped the three. The man named Dean stepped close and hissed in his ear. "You makin' a mistake, boy."

Miller knew it. He dropped the four.

The man's friend pointed at Miller and mouthed something he couldn't make out.

Miller stepped back from the table and rested the bottom of his cue on the floor. "Let's make this easy. I have seven more dollars in my pocket. That makes twelve altogether. You want to fight for it here or outside?"

The man smirked.

Miller dropped the five. He missed on the six, and the man moved in and made a tough shot, then ran the seven and the eight. The nine lay up in the corner by the pocket.

The man stepped close to Miller. "Think you so fucking smart." He leaned over the table and dropped the nine.

Miller watched the man scoop up the ten dollars. He pointed at Miller. "Loser racks. New game for seven bucks."

Miller turned away.

They turned after him. He reached the door, but the man's friend was there before him.

The voice from across the room came back. "I said knock it off, Dean."

"We ain't doing nothin'."

"He's just a kid."

"He's gotta learn."

The voice said, "I think he did. I said to knock it off."

Miller took advantage of the moment to get himself out the door. He ran for the truck and no one seemed to be following him and he yanked the door open and slid into the cab.

Johnny was sitting on the passenger side.

Miller didn't want to slow down and he jammed the key in and started the truck and pulled away. Johnny sat calmly and didn't say a thing.

Miller looked over. She had her hands tucked into the tiny pockets on her tiny jacket. He had no idea what to do, so he said, "I can drop you somewhere."

Johnny shook her head. She looked small and sad and cold. "Anywhere."

Miller drove. "What do you mean anywhere?"

"Look, I'm sorry I got in your truck. I just wanted…"

The blower whined and spat out some air.

"I wanted something different."

So did Miller.

Johnny shrugged as if she was trying to stuff more of herself down into the tiny jacket. "No luck finding your pa, huh?"

He shook his head. "How'd you know which truck was mine?"

Johnny looked out the windshield at the headlights on the road. "Only one I didn't know."

Miller turned the wheel into a curve of the road. "What if it wasn't mine?"

"It'd be somebody I didn't know."

The truck glided through the dark. Miller said, "Look, I like you, and I'm sure—"

She put a finger to his lips and he stopped. When she took her hand away she said, "I think you better just take me back."

Miller did. And when Johnny slid out of the truck she didn't look back.

16

MILLER SQUINTED through the windshield. The road was a dark and twisting tunnel. Pa was a phantom, a flicker of light ahead that disappeared behind every curve. Jeannie was a hand reaching out to him through a mist. He pressed on.

Miller knew he should go home. But there were questions in his mind he couldn't answer. If he could find those men and settle whatever score his pa had with them, that would protect Jeannie. If he could find somebody who could tell him something about what was going on, that would help Jeannie.

He let the truck glide into the parking lot of the Ghost House Saloon. This place was almost as remote as the last, a small structure at the edge of a clump of houses in a place with no name.

A sliver of moonlight lit the enclave. Rumor said that the Ghost House had been haunted before it was a bar, when it was home to two brothers who were lost in the Vietnam war. The story was that the spirits of the brothers had come back to the house to grieve. But the brothers' parents couldn't face living in the house without the sons, and they sold the place and moved on. The ghostly siblings stayed, grieving and waiting for their parents, who would never return. When the house became a bar, it inherited the spirits.

Miller didn't believe much in ghosts, though he'd heard tales of them all his life and knew he was supposed to believe. Tonight he would be happy enough to find one if it was the spirit of his pa.

He moved the bench seat of the truck back and bent over to reach underneath. His hand closed on the envelope he knew would be wedged beneath a spring. He pulled the envelope out and removed the single bill that was inside, a twenty, and tucked that into his wallet.

The act of removing the bill drained some of the confidence from Miller. The money was disappearing. He was getting nowhere. Jeannie was home alone. The men looking for his pa would return. His will to go into the bar was slipping away.

He cocked his head toward the sliver of moon and tried to let his thoughts drift away like water in a stream. Then he let his feet lead. His heart wouldn't take him.

The Ghost House was no Rudy's, and nothing had changed much since Miller's pa had brought him here when he was a kid. The walls inside the house had been carved open to make a space for a bar down the length of one side and tables against the opposite wall under a window. It still looked mostly like a home. There was a tiny kitchen at the back of the house, and the old family bathroom at the end of the bar. But it smelled like a saloon, beer and smoke and must.

Half a dozen people sat at the bar, all of them absently watching a TV that hung behind it. There was no music and there were no pool tables. Miller could not hear anyone talking. They all just sat facing the TV with the colors from it flashing over their faces.

No one at the bar turned to look when Miller walked the length of the room. A man older than his pa sat on a stool behind the bar, and he glanced at Miller and nodded once, then turned back to the TV.

Miller didn't recognize anyone. Not the man behind the bar. None of the faces in the wash of light from behind the bar. No one he knew from the days his pa would bring him here.

He felt an urgency to be home, to see Jeannie and know that she was all right. He turned for the door. When he'd nearly reached it, the man on a stool at the end stood and laid a hand on Miller's shoulder.

Miller's heart thudded.

The man was grinning. "Ain't you Zeb Brenning's son?"

Miller looked at the man and his muscles relaxed. "Cousin Rebel?"

Rebel was not his cousin. He was pa's cousin. But Miller had only ever known him as cousin Rebel.

"Damn, boy," Rebel said. "Lemme see you." He stood back. "Last time you was what—" He held a hand out at about the height of Miller's chest. "About this big?"

Miller guessed that was about right.

"Now look at you. Almost as tall as me."

Taller, Miller thought, but he didn't say it.

Some of the others had turned from the TV and were looking at them. Rebel gave one of the men a long look, and the man turned away. He clapped Miller's shoulder. "Come on, boy, I'll buy you a beer."

Miller shook his head. "I need to talk to you."

Rebel looked at the split in Miller's lip and the bruises on his face. "I guess you do."

Miller looked to the door. Rebel reached for a bottle of beer on the bar and picked it up and finished it with a long pull. He set the empty bottle down, and they went out into the chill of the night.

Rebel hunkered into his coat and scanned the cars in the lot and pointed. "That Zeb's truck?"

Miller stuffed his hands into his pockets. "Yeah."

"He here? I wanna talk to him."

Miller's mind skipped a groove. "You're looking for pa?"

"Yeah." Rebel turned, and Miller's memory caught hold and he remembered his pa and cousin Rebel, when pa was distilling up in the hills behind Rebel's house. The two of them were tight. Rebel had scared Miller some then. He had thick arms and a thick neck and he drank a lot and tried to wrestle playfully with Miller, but Rebel was too big for that and Miller had been too small. Miller had tried to keep his distance.

Rebel looked about the same now but a little older. He needed a shave and new coat. Neither of those seemed to bother him none.

Rebel pointed a finger at Miller. "Zeb said he needed to lay low for a spell. But I ain't seen him in near two weeks. He out at the house now?"

Miller shook his head.

Rebel put a big hand under Miller's jaw and lifted it to

look better at the bruises and busted lip. "Damn, boy. He do that to you?"

Miller pulled his head away. "Pa ain't home."

"That ain't no kind of answer. What do you mean he ain't home?"

"He ain't been home."

Rebel hunched against the cold and his big shoulders rolled. "How long? How long he ain't been home?"

"Same as you said. Two weeks."

Rebel scuffed a boot in the dirt.

Miller said, "Why'd he need to lay low?"

"What do I know? I ain't seen him."

"But you know something."

Rebel spat once in the weeds. "Wish I did." He spat again. "Why'd you get in a fight?"

Miller shrugged. "Why not?"

Rebel grunted. He looked out at the truck again. "How's you and Jeannie and your mamma gettin' on without Zeb there?"

"Ma ain't there neither."

Rebel's bulky shoulders jumped. "The hell you mean, she ain't there? Her and Zeb run off together?"

Miller almost laughed, but it wasn't funny. "No. Ma's been gone longer."

Rebel stepped closer. "How long?"

"Summer." The word came out like air escaping a tire.

"Who's been looking after you and Jeannie?"

Miller tried to straighten his shoulders. "I am. And Jeannie can look after herself. She's grown."

Rebel twisted his head once, hard, like he was trying to crack his neck. "Damn, what the *hell* is going on?"

Miller's jaw tensed when he tried to speak. "Some men come to the house."

"Men? What men? When?"

"Today."

"What'd they want?"

"They wanted pa."

"What'd you tell 'em?"

"He wasn't there. I run 'em off."

Rebel's shoulders wouldn't stop moving, a mass of agitated energy, waking up. "You run 'em off?"

Miller nodded.

"How many men?"

"Two."

"What'd they say they wanted Zeb for?"

"They didn't."

Rebel's shoulders had settled some, but he was still a looming wall of energy. "These men. They treat you well enough?"

Miller's eyes dropped. "No." A moment passed, and he added, "I showed them the shotgun."

Rebel craned his neck. "You use it?"

"Almost. I think pa was making shine again."

Rebel didn't say anything.

"Was he?"

"Your pa wanted you to know what he was doing, he would'a told you."

Miller felt it again, the fear he'd had of cousin Rebel when he was younger.

Rebel clapped Miller's shoulder again. "What'd the men who came to the house look like?"

"One of them had something wrong with his beard." Miller touched his face. "It wouldn't grow right." His hand went to his side. "The other had a pistol in his belt, had a white butt on it."

Rebel looked up at the moon, ran a hand through his hair, looked back at Miller. "We got to get you out of that house. You and Jeannie."

"That ain't something we was hoping to do."

"Listen, boy. You think you're growed up, but you ain't that growed up yet. These here men lookin' for your daddy ain't gonna go easy on you because you're young. We got to get you and Jeannie out."

Miller clenched his fingers, unclenched them. "Who are they?"

Rebel shook his head.

"Who?"

"I don't know. We got to find that out. But I know the kind of men your daddy dealt with. We got to get you and Jeannie out of there."

Gears turned in Miller's head. "I sent them to Munson."

"What?"

"I told those men that pa was working at a sawmill over in Munson. Then I come out tonight looking for them, but they might be over in Munson."

"You come looking for them?"

"I didn't know what else to do. Figured I'd come to them before they come back for me."

Rebel grinned. "Damn, boy, you sure are Zeb's son."

Miller frowned. It wasn't something he wanted to hear.

Rebel said, "I didn't know there was a sawmill in Munson."

"As far as I know, there ain't."

Rebel's eyes crinkled. "They come back, they'll take it out on you." He reached to his inside jacket pocket and took out a pack of cigarettes and lit one. The smoke curled up from his face and wafted into the moonlight.

Miller said, "What'd you want pa for? Whyn't you come to the house looking for him?"

Rebel squinted against the smoke. "Your pa and I had some business. But your ma never liked me comin' around much."

Rebel smoked some and Miller asked him, "Can you help me find pa?"

Rebel squeezed a tight stream of smoke out between his lips. "I'm gonna try." He smoked some more, and then he seemed to come to some sort of decision. He dropped the cigarette butt to the dirt and stepped on it. "You go home and pack some things. Wake Jeannie and have her do the same. I'll come by first thing in the daylight and get you."

Miller's hands flexed.

Rebel saw it. "I know it ain't what you want to do. But this ain't about wantin'. It's about what you got to do. Until we find your pa and get this figured out."

Miller did not move.

Rebel pressed a hand onto Miller's shoulder again. "Think about Jeannie."

He had been. He'd thought about the men in the woods and what he knew they would have done to Jeannie. About the men who'd come to the house looking for his pa. He wanted to tell Rebel what he'd done, that he'd killed two men two nights before and the act of it was still hanging tight over him and clouding his judgement.

But that was a secret he kept for Jeannie. If he went away, there would be no one left for her.

The sliver of moonlight on the horizon struggled to cut through a passing cloud. Pa was a light fading in the distance. Jeannie was a hand reaching to him through a mist. Miller turned and walked away.

17

MILLER PULLED the twenty from his wallet and put it back into the envelope. He bent and tucked that under the spring beneath the seat. Then he started for home.

He drove slowly, thinking about what he would say to Jeannie.

Miller came into the house and hung his coat on a peg by the door and went to the kitchen. He reached up to the high cupboard, way in the back where pa kept the quart jar of money. The jar was painted black, and Miller and Jeannie weren't supposed to get into it or know it was there, but it hadn't been a secret from them for a long time. They didn't get into the money for fear that pa would find out. But now with pa gone, Miller thought of the money as his own.

He took the jar to the kitchen table and emptied it and began counting. When he had the bills counted out into stacks and was deciding what to do with it, Jeannie's bedroom door opened and she padded into the kitchen. Bailey followed her, his toenails clicking on the wooden floor.

"That's pa's money," Jeannie said.

Miller looked up. "Pa's not here. It's ours now."

Jeannie sat at the table and looked over the piles. "How much?"

"Couple hundred. A little more."

"That all we got?"

"That I know of."

"Don't sound like much."

"It's not. I figure the electric bill's gonna come soon. I don't know how we can pay that in cash. We could leave it go. Probably be a while before they shut it off."

Jeannie worked at something under her fingernail. "What all other bills is there?"

"I don't even know."

"There's gas and groceries."

"Yeah. That's what we've been spending it on so far."

Jeannie stopped working on her fingernail. "How long's that gonna last?"

"I figure we can make a go of it for a while, if we have to."

Jeannie pulled at the ends of the blanket around her shoulders and wrapped it tighter. Miller watched her, then he slid some money across the table to Jeannie. "None of that might not matter pretty soon. You remember pa's cousin Rebel?"

Jeannie's face scrunched up. "Rebel? I don't want to remember him."

"Yeah, he used to scare me some too."

Jeannie looked at the money in front of her.

Miller pointed. "Take it."

"What for?"

"We can't leave it here. And we might need it."

She reached a hand out and touched the bills, like they were something foreign she was trying to figure out.

"Keep that for you. Put it someplace safe, someplace you can get to. If you can, don't put it all in one place."

Jeannie pulled her hand back. "Why are you doing this? Why don't we just keep it in the jar?"

Miller folded the bills he'd pushed to Jeannie and tucked them into her hand. He took some of the other bills and folded them and put them in his wallet. "I'm putting a little back in the jar. And I'm moving the jar. We're going to hide it out in the woodpile. I'll show you where." He tucked two twenties into the jar and screwed the lid on. He felt like a squirrel, hiding his nuts all around so that he could find one if he needed it. It seemed silly, but it made him feel safer.

Jeannie's fingers twitched around the folded bills. "What are you doing? What's happening?" The pitch of her voice climbed upward.

"It's all right."

"What do you mean we can't leave the money here? Why not?"

"Rebel's coming."

Jeannie blinked. "Here?"

"Yes."

"Why?"

Miller pushed the jar to the side and looked across at the table at Jeannie. "I saw Rebel tonight. He's looking for pa too. He didn't know pa was gone." He gave that a moment to sink in, then went on. "Rebel didn't know about ma either. I told him about the men who came here looking for pa, and he said we have to get out of here in case they come back."

"No."

"They'll come back."

"You ran them off once."

"Barely. Look, it's not going to be safe here."

"No. I don't want to go. I don't want to go with cousin Rebel."

"I don't like it either. But if they come back when I'm not here—"

"I can use the gun."

"I know you can. But even if I was here, I don't know if I'd be able to…"

Jeannie glared at Miller and he thought she must believe he was weak.

"Those men in the woods," he said. "They were going to…"

"I know what they were gonna do." She snatched her hand with the money under her blanket and stood up. "I could go stay with Rubylee."

Miller shook his head.

"She'd take me in. Mister and Missus Slocum would. I've been going over there."

"That's what I don't like about it. People know you've been going there. They could find you."

"Why would they want to find me?"

"I don't know. To find pa. To get to him."

Jeannie calmly smoothed the blanket around her shoulders and looked Miller in the eye. "Pa's dead."

Miller breathed. "Maybe. But those men aren't. And they think pa is alive. They'll come back."

"Slocums' is better than with cousin Rebel."

Slow it down, Miller thought. Don't push Jeannie. You'll lose her. "We have to stay together."

"You could come to the Slocoms' too."

"No."

They looked at each other, then Miller said, "We'll be safer at Rebel's. He can help us find pa." He sighed. "Or what happened to pa. Rebel can help protect us if those men come."

"They could find us at cousin Rebel's just as soon as anywhere."

Miller had expected that Jeannie might cry, but she kept surprising him. She stood her ground. Her face stayed dry. Miller breathed. Slow it down. Don't lose her. "Rebel's will be safer. He can help us."

"We could go somewhere. We could sleep in the truck. We could look for ma. If she ain't dead yet too."

"We don't have enough money to stay anywhere for very long. And Rebel is the only family I know of."

"We could look for ma."

"I hear you. But I don't know where to start. And we don't have much money for it."

"Maybe we get cousin Rebel to help us look for pa but we go out on our own. We sleep in the truck. Move around."

Miller felt something like pride for his sister. And also a fear for her that he struggled to get a hold of. "Maybe. We don't have much time to sort that out."

"When's Rebel coming?"

"Daybreak. You need to pack some things. Not much. Just what you can carry."

Jeannie frowned. "What about the house?"

"We'll lock it up. It's all we can do."

"The pipes'll freeze."

"I'll turn the water off. Drain what I can and leave the taps open." He looked at the potbelly stove. "Build the fire hot. Heat up the house as much as we can before we go. It's not freezing every night."

"That's a waste of wood. Just do the other stuff."

Miller nodded.

Jeannie looked at the dog. "What about Bailey?"

"Fill his bowl. Put out lots of water. He's a dog. He can come and go. He'll take care of himself."

"He'll eat it all if you put out a lot of food."

"Then don't. He'll hunt when he gets hungry. He'll have to."

Jeannie bent and patted Bailey on the head and spoke to him. Her voice broke. "I don't want to go."

"Neither do I."

She patted Bailey some more. "Does cousin Rebel still live at that place with all the land?"

Miller shrugged. "I guess so. I don't know."

Jeannie stopped stroking the dog and straightened herself. "And he'll be here in the morning?"

"First thing."

"Everybody wants to take us away."

They did. Miller picked up the jar with the twenties in it. "I'm putting this in the back of the woodpile, right by Bailey's door. I'm telling you in case we need it."

"We'll need it," Jeannie said.

Miller knew she was right. He didn't tell her that. Instead he said, "Just pack."

18

MILLER PULLED his jacket on. It was cold in the house and he felt his breath come out in steamy wisps.

Fingers of light reached over the hills and extended down through the windows of the Brenning house. Bailey was outside snuffling at the base of a tree. Neither Miller nor Jeannie had gotten much sleep.

Jeannie stacked wood into the potbelly stove. Miller opened a kitchen cupboard door and said, "What should we have for breakfast?" He pulled out a jar. "How about peanut butter?"

Jeannie gave him a look that crinkled her eyes but would not break into a smile. Miller pushed the peanut butter back into the cupboard and swung the refrigerator door open. "How about we finish the eggs instead?"

"Eh." She maneuvered another piece of wood into the stove.

Miller scrambled the eggs and made toast and coffee and set out butter and jam. He put the eggs in a big bowl and set them on the table.

Jeannie was in the other room on the couch. Miller looked out to her and said, "It's ready."

She stared out the window and didn't come.

He tried again. "Breakfast."

"I'm not hungry."

"Me either. But we've got to eat."

"I said I'm not hungry."

He sat. "I don't know what we'll be having to eat. Better get something now while we can."

She still didn't come. Miller piled eggs onto his plate and took a bite with some toast. He poured coffee and took a sip.

Jeannie finally rose from the couch and came slowly to the table. She sighed heavily and forked some eggs onto her plate. She looked at them but did not eat.

Miller pushed the salt over. Jeannie made a face and pushed the salt away. "There's already enough."

"How do you know? You haven't tasted them yet."

"You always put too much in."

Miller chewed and swallowed, licked a finger. "That I do."

He ate some more and Jeannie hooked a small bite of egg onto the end of her fork and looked at it. She ate it with a corner of toast. Then she set her fork down.

"Eat," Miller said.

Jeannie folded her arms together. "Everything is screwed up."

The look she gave Miller was angry and piercing. He didn't like it. "It's not my fault."

"Well it sure as hell ain't my fault."

He set his fork down. Washed down a bite with some

coffee. "You're right. It's not your fault either. You feel better about it now?"

The frown on Jeannie's face deepened. "That's it? That's all you got to say?"

"What do you want me to say?"

"Say you'll do something. Besides just sit there and eat all the eggs."

Miller pushed his chair back from the table. "It's the best we can do right now."

"Running away ain't the best we can do. Runnin' off with pa's cousin Rebel sure ain't the best we can do."

Miller tried for patience, but it was not coming easily to him. He said, "We talked about this."

"That's what it is," Jeannie said. "Just talk."

Miller picked up his coffee cup, lifted it, looked at it, felt something bubbling up inside him that he tried to keep down. He placed the cup back down carefully and laid his hands on the table. "What do you expect me to do?"

Jeannie's frown burned slowly. Miller knew it was a fuse. He tried to stop himself, but the heat had risen in him. "What?" he said. "I didn't hear you. Did you say something?" He put a hand behind an ear and tilted it toward Jeannie.

Jeannie moved closer to tears, or screaming. He didn't know which.

"This is it," Miller said. "This is what I'm doing. What I've been doing. There's nothing else we can do. Get yourself right with it."

Jeannie very quietly pushed her plate away. "Fuck you."

Miller slapped his hands on the table and pushed himself up. The breakfast plates rattled and coffee slopped from his cup. "That's just great. Fuck you. Just great." He kicked his chair away. "Clean up the dishes when you're done."

"You clean them up," Jeannie said, and she got up and left.

Miller went to his room, to the backpack and gym bag he had packed with his things. He worked hard trying to cool his thoughts, to think of something to say to Jeannie that would make her feel better. The words didn't come.

He looked around his room for what else he might be able to fit into one of the bags. He heard Jeannie filling Bailey's food bowl in the kitchen, and he watched through his open bedroom door as she got bowls down from the cupboards and filled them with water and set them on the floor.

When Miller carried his bag and backpack out to set them by the front door, Jeannie stepped silently around him and went out in the yard and called for Bailey.

He cleaned up the breakfast dishes. Made two sandwiches of leftover toast and eggs and stuffed them into his backpack. He finished his coffee and dried the dishes and watched Jeannie out in the yard with Bailey.

When he was done, Miller went out and stood at the porch railing to watch Jeannie. She looked up at Miller and patted Bailey's head. "Can't we take him with us?"

The look on her face made Miller second-guess what they were doing. His choice. What they were doing because he'd decided. Not Jeannie's choice. "Maybe," he said. "We'll ask Rebel when he gets here."

Jeannie patted Bailey's head some more. "It's going to be OK, boy. We'll be back soon. We'll take care of you."

Bailey raised his head to absorb the attention Jeannie was giving him. "There's nothing else my brother can do. He's kind of a doofus."

The muscles in Miller's neck tensed. He didn't know if Jeannie was playing the game. If she was, his heart wasn't willing to join her in it. He held his tongue. No words were better than coarse ones.

Then came the sound of a car slowing as it pulled off the road and started up the drive toward the house. Jeannie saw it and turned.

"Jeannie," Miller called. "Get up here."

She did, and Bailey followed her onto the porch.

The car stopped at the split in the drive that went either to their house or the Jacksons'. Miller instinctively took a slow step backward toward the door, where the shotgun was propped against the wall on the other side.

The car's engine was still running and no one got out. It didn't look right. Rebel would come in a truck. There'd probably be a shivering dog in the back. This vehicle was a four-door, black and sleek and new. Not enough dirt on the windshield or fenders. Not much mud on the tires. No room for a gun rack in the back window. A city car.

"Jeannie," Miller said. And then a woman stepped out of the car.

The woman looked young. Miller thought maybe thirty. She had long dark hair and wore jeans and city boots and a snug-fitting jacket that looked good on her but wouldn't keep her warm if she had to be outside for long. She pulled a yellow knit hat onto her head and started up toward the house.

"Who's that?" Jeannie said.

Miller shook his head.

Before the woman reached the house, Miller shouted out, "Hello."

The woman stopped and looked up at the porch to Miller and Jeannie and Bailey. She turned both ways and scanned left and right and her gaze lingered on the house next door, then she turned back. "This is the Brennings'?"

Miller didn't answer. Jeannie moved a step closer to him.

The woman came toward them. Miller could see that she was maybe younger than he had thought. Twenties. Pretty. A black over-the-shoulder bag rode gently on one hip and she held a cell phone in her hand.

The woman stopped at the base of the porch stairs and looked up at Miller and Jeannie. "Hello," she said. She held out a laminated ID card. "My name is Anna Bostwick. I'm with Child Services."

Jeannie stepped behind her brother until she had nearly disappeared. Anna Bostwick put her attention so squarely on Miller that he felt his face warm. He did not come forward or reach down for the card.

The woman held her arm stretched out in front of her to empty air, then withdrew the hand and tucked the card back into the bag. "You're Albert and Jeannette?"

"Miller," he said. Jeannie was silent, so Miller added for her, "Jeannie."

"OK." The woman smiled brightly, as if she was posing. "Are your parents home? I'd like to speak with them."

Miller felt Jeannie hovering behind his shoulder. "They're off right now," he said.

"OK." The woman stood calmly and pushed dark hair over her shoulder and smoothed the strands behind an ear. She smiled again. "Can you tell me when they might be back?"

Miller shrugged. "Sometime later."

The woman was patient. Her smile never wavered. It unnerved Miller. He said, "Why do you want to talk to them?"

The woman peered over Miller's shoulder, then her eyes went down to Bailey. "May I come up?"

"Depends."

The woman nodded. "It does." She tucked her phone away into a pocket. "Look, we can do this now, or I can come back later and do it. Usually there's two of us, but we've got some people out with the flu. So if we do it now you just get me. If we come back later there will be two of us."

Miller didn't like it, but she was convincing. "What do you want?"

"I just need to ask you a few questions. Nothing is going to happen to anybody."

Jeannie stepped out from behind Miller. "You promise?"

"I do." She swished a hand over her chest. "Cross my heart."

Jeannie's eyes flicked to Miller, to the woman, back to Miller. The woman watched her, then said to Jeannie, "You'll hold the dog?"

Jeannie said, "He does what he wants."

The woman took a step forward, and Bailey put his head down and growled. The woman stopped. Her hand drifted slowly into the bag at her side and came out with a dog biscuit. She held it up for Miller to see. "May I?"

He shrugged.

The woman set the treat on a step and backed away. Bailey grabbed up the biscuit and scampered to the far end of the porch with it.

Anna Bostwick was smarter than Miller had thought. And more prepared.

Then the social worker reached into her bag again and pulled out her business card again. This time Miller took it.

Jeannie reached into Miller's fingers and plucked the card out.

"Ma'am," Miller said. "Why are you here?"

"Annabella," Jeannie said, reading the card. "It says your name is Annabella."

The woman smiled at Jeannie. "You can call me Anna."

Miller said, "What do you want?"

Anna Bostwick looked Miller in the eye. She was even prettier up close than Miller had realized. Her cheeks were flushed from the cold air, and her skin looked soft and free of makeup. It made him uncomfortable to notice those things about her and he looked away. When his eyes came back she was still there, quietly regarding him.

He remembered the marks on his face. The bruises were fading, and the lip was healing up. But the woman was close and had probably seen what was left of the injuries, and they felt to Miller like hot red flashes on his cheeks. He readied a lie—that he'd been running and got caught in some branches, or that they were felling dead trees for firewood and one of the limbs broke away and whacked him—but the woman didn't ask.

Instead, she said simply, "The county sometimes performs welfare checks as a service to the community. This is a standard procedure, and—"

"Someone called you?"

Anna looked at Miller, then closed her eyes once slowly and reopened them. "Yes, someone called the office."

Miller's attention went across the way to the Jacksons' house. Anna followed his gaze and said, "I can't tell you who called. Children's Services is not allowed to—"

"Children's Services? I'm not a child."

"No." Anna shook her head, but she did not look away from Miller. "You're not. That's not what it means. It's just the name of the county office. That's nothing to do with who you are."

Her beauty was striking. So was her poise. Miller didn't know what to do with that.

"I'm just here to make a preliminary assessment," Anna said. "To make sure there is proper adult supervision."

The words rolled through Miller's head like stones.

"I'm not making those judgments about you, whether you're an adult or not. I know it's not the same for everyone. That's just the way the system works."

Miller stood without speaking. Anna did not let her gaze wander from him.

This woman made Miller feel like both a child and an adult at the same time. He didn't like it, but he liked the way Anna Bostwick was looking at him. And he didn't like that, because he knew it softened him. "What do you need to know?" he said.

"Your parents," she said. "Where are they? Can I talk to them?"

"Pa's working at a sawmill over in Munson. He keeps odd hours. Has some long shifts. He'll be back when they let him off."

Anna took a small pad of notepaper from her pocket and wrote briefly on it. "Munson? That's pretty far away?"

"It's a stretch," Miller said. "It's where the work is."

"OK." She nodded. "What's the name of the sawmill?"

Miller worked to keep his expression flat. "Pa didn't say."

"Do you have an address? A phone number? How do you contact him if you need something?"

"Pa doesn't carry a phone. They don't let you call them while they're working."

"OK. So he just leaves for work and then comes back, and that's all you know?"

"It's over in Munson."

"You said that. You don't know anything else?"

"That's right. It ain't that unusual around here. Lots of folks work out a ways and they come and go as they need to."

Anna wrote a few more hasty items on her notepad. "When do you expect him back?"

"Hard to say. Sometimes they sleep over. It's a long drive home in the dark."

Anna held the pen but had not written more. Her smile remained in place. "And when he does come home?"

"Late. Way after dark. Leaves real early."

"So you don't see your father very much."

Miller worked to keep his voice flat. "Not when there's work."

Anna wrote something. "And your mother?"

"She's visiting family."

Anna waited, then said. "Where? How can I contact her?"

Miller shook his head. "We're estranged."

"Estranged?"

"It means we don't talk to that part of the family."

"I know what it means. Why would she visit if you're estranged?"

"It's ma's family. She's not estranged."

Miller saw the question on Anna's face before she asked it. "Pa don't like us going over there."

Anna wrote very briefly. "When do you expect your mother to return?"

Miller shrugged. "She doesn't drive."

Anna curled a lock of hair behind one ear. "What does that mean?"

"They have to give her a ride home. We'll be fine until then."

"I don't doubt that," Anna said. She stepped back to look at both Miller and Jeannie. "What about school?"

Miller shrugged. "What about it?"

Anna Bostwick's finger tapped against the side of her bag. Then it stopped. "OK, here's what happens. The county is not going to let this go until someone has spoken to one of your parents. That could be me or someone else. But it'll have to be someone, and soon." She looked from Jeannie to Miller. "I could take you with me now. Call for someone else to come out and help if I need to. That's my judgment call, OK? I can do that."

Miller's mind raced. It went nowhere he could fathom.

"But I'm not going to do that right now. Not yet." She stepped sideways to get a better look at Jeannie. "I'd like to talk to your sister for a bit before I decide that."

No one said a thing.

Finally, Miller said, "You mean without me."

"If you don't mind."

Miller's head was shaking no, but Jeannie bobbed her head yes. She looked at her brother. "I can do it."

Miller clomped down from the porch and walked in a wide circle around the house and sat on a corner of the woodpile.

19

MILLER REGRETTED leaving them alone. He trusted Jeannie to protect their secrets, but Anna Bostwick was good, and lies were slippery things that came easily undone. He thought Jeannie could lie well enough about ma and pa, but dead men were a harder secret to keep.

He wondered if he should have told Anna about Rebel. If Rebel would really come for them. If Anna and the county people would let him and Jeannie be if Rebel took them in. If Rebel would do that.

Then he wondered if Jeannie would tell Anna Bostwick about Rebel, or if she already had.

He could not stay settled sitting on the woodpile so he got up and roamed the open yard and grounds surrounding the house. He moved some wood from the chopping block to the pile under the lean-to. He gathered some downed branches for tinder. Over his shoulder as he moved he stole glimpses of Jeannie and Anna Bostwick on the porch.

He walked down the slope toward the drive and looked closer at Anna Bostwick's car, which had no official markings on it. He wondered if it was hers or belonged to the county. It seemed the type of car a county worker would get to use for official business—clean, dark, compact, and urban. It also seemed like the kind of car a woman like Anna would drive. He decided it didn't matter much, and he looked once more up at Jeannie and Anna on the porch.

They sat together in a set of old wicker chairs, Anna with her coat pulled tight around her and looking cold, Jeannie hunched forward with one hand down petting Bailey's head. Miller was aware that they had been talking for a long time, long enough that it had begun to feel awkward. He roamed the yard trying to find something to focus on.

When Miller had had enough and was ready to reassert himself into the conversation, Anna's voice came out to him before he could act on his decision.

"Miller." She'd remembered not to call him Albert, like it said on the paperwork she'd read from. That was something. He turned and saw Anna standing on the porch waving him in.

Miller closed on the house and climbed the porch steps. Jeannie and Anna rose together as he neared them, and he stood feeling like an outsider as he watched the easy motions between the two of them. Anna shivered and hugged her jacket close to her body, and Miller briefly thought to offer her his coat before he stopped himself.

Anna Bostwick said to Miller, "I'm going to leave you my number."

"We already have it. On the card." Miller put a hand to

his pocket, then realized that Jeannie had taken the card. "Well, she has it."

"No, my personal number."

Miller waited. "What's on the card you gave us?"

"My work number. With the county. You can call me there. And you can leave a message if I'm not there, or talk to someone else if you wait on the line. But I'm going to give you my own number."

Miller remembered her walking up to the house with a phone in her hand. "Why would you do that?"

"It's discretionary."

Miller shifted from one foot to the other, and a board in the porch floor squeaked loudly.

"It means I can decide—"

"I know what it means."

Anna smiled brightly at Miller. "Of course you do. This is my discretion. I'm giving you my number."

Miller looked around as if he'd lost something. Then he said, "There's nothing to write it on. You want to write it on the back of your card?" He glanced at Jeannie to let her know that he expected her to hand over the card.

Jeannie didn't offer Miller the card. She shook her head instead and said, "Just put it in the phone, like a normal person."

The words *simpleton* and *doofus* floated into Miller's head, but he caught them before they could escape his mouth. Now was not the time to play the game. He reached to his pocket, then remembered. "Jeannie, you have the phone?"

It was already in Jeannie's hand.

Anna recited her number, and Jeannie touched it into the phone.

A truck rumbled past on the road below, and Miller remembered Rebel. The thought of him here with Anna made him sweat.

"OK," Miller said. "We've got your number."

Anna put the smile on him again. "Someone will have to come back. I'll make sure it's me." The smile put heat into Miller's cheeks again.

Then Anna Bostwick walked carefully down the porch steps in her city shoes and when she reached the bottom she twisted her head as she walked and said, "Be careful." She hugged her jacket to her ribs and hurried down to her car.

They watched her drive away. Miller squinted at the vehicle as it pulled onto the road. "Been more people to the house the last couple a days than in a month of Wednesdays."

Jeannie snickered. "It's Sundays, doofus."

"Wednesdays is the same thing, mental midget."

Her eyes went up and down the road. "Everyone except who we were expecting."

"Yeah."

Jeannie rubbed her nose. "You didn't tell her about cousin Rebel."

"I didn't. Did you?"

"No."

He put his hands in his pockets. "Seems like you liked her."

"She's better than cousin Rebel."

Miller rocked on his feet. "She'd take us away."

"She couldn't."

"I don't know. She could get help, she needed it. Might not need it."

Jeannie gave him a look. "You run off them two men that come here lookin' for daddy, but you'd let a woman get the better of you?"

"It's different."

"How's it different? Maybe you're the one that likes her."

"No, that ain't it."

"Then what?"

Miller rocked again. "Can't say. It's just different. I'd need you."

"For what?"

"If she came back. To help with her."

"Help?"

"Getting rid of her. I don't think she'd believe me. You might be able to convince her."

"Convince her of what?"

Miller thought about it. Convince Anna that they weren't lying? So he said, "What's best for us."

"You mean that she won't take us away."

"I guess she already doesn't want to do that."

Jeannie looked at the road again. "Cousin Rebel's gonna take us away."

"That's different."

"How's it different?"

"Our choice. We're takin' the truck. We can leave when we want to."

"You think he'll let us do that?"

Miller hunched his shoulders. "He'll have to, if it's what we want. He won't want to keep us for long, anyway. Not used to having people like us around."

"You mean having kids around."

"I guess so."

They watched the road together. Jeannie said, "I don't feel much like a kid anymore."

Miller didn't answer. He figured she had that about right.

"You think Rebel's coming?"

"I don't know. Probably. Said he was."

"So we just stand here and wait? See if those men come back? Ask them in for tea and what they want with daddy?"

"No."

"Then what now?"

Miller didn't want there to be a what now. He didn't want there to be anything they had to do. He wanted to sit down and feel safe and for everybody else to go away. He wanted ma to come back, and he wanted to know what had happened to pa. He almost wanted pa back, but that didn't seem quite like what he was feeling. He wanted nothing to worry about. He wanted to feel at peace. But that's not how it was. "Now we load our things in the truck."

"And if Rebel doesn't come?"

Clouds were moving in slowly from the west. Miller watched the dark spot they made on the horizon. "He'll come."

20

MILLER CLOSED the door, and they carried their bags to the truck. It was a tight fit to get everything into the cab.

Each of them had a small gym bag and a backpack. Miller didn't know how long they'd be gone or what they would need or even if they'd leave Rebel and end up somewhere else. He didn't know what to take, so he didn't take much. Some clothes, a sweatshirt, long underwear. Boots, hat, gloves. He wondered what was in Jeannie's bags, but he didn't ask.

Miller tilted the truck's bench seat forward and they rearranged the tools and rags and tie-down straps and pieces of rope scattered there. They pushed the backpacks behind the seat into the spaces they'd carved out.

Then Jeannie stacked the gym bags on top of each other in the middle of the bench seat. Miller got in and tried the stick shift. It hung up on the bags when he tried to pull the shift down into the bottom gears. Jeannie turned the bags sideways and punched them in so they would have enough room to sit, and the stick shift cleared them.

Bailey had been watching while they worked, but something out in the yard caught his attention and he wandered off to investigate.

Miller considered the bags. "These might be better on the floor over there. Under your feet."

"It's dirty down there."

"We could clean it out."

"You could. I don't want my bag on the floor."

"OK."

"It's gross."

"OK."

"And I don't want my feet all tangled up in them."

"I said OK."

Jeannie glared at Miller. "I heard you." She stretched her neck to look behind the seat and poked a hand back there. "There's room for a little more. I'm gonna go get some things."

Miller let her go and sat in the truck by himself and let the quiet surround him.

Jeannie came back a few minutes later carrying an extra pair of gloves, a book, a flashlight, and a paper sack that was folded over on the top.

"What's in the sack?"

She held the top open. "Food."

Miller looked in. There was the box of crackers, some cans of soup, and the packaged cupcakes he'd gotten for her.

Jeannie folded the top of the sack back over again and said, "They can look you up."

"What?"

"They can find you."

"Who can?"

"The county people. Anna and them. If there's a reason. They can get a judge to open up court records and give them access to legal documents and stuff."

"Court records?"

"Like birth certificates and stuff."

"She told you that?"

Jeannie didn't have to say yes.

"Why would they want to do that?"

"I don't know. To find your family or something."

"Our family? We ain't got no family."

"Mamma has family."

"None that I ever met."

"But you know she does. She had a sister."

"Aunt Fish."

"Yeah."

Miller stretched his legs out as best he could under the truck's steering column. "How come we never met her?"

"You've heard mamma talk."

"Not for a long time. I figure Aunt Fish is dead or ma don't know where she is. I never was sure she was real."

Jeannie stared out the windshield with Miller. She tucked her bag of food up on the dashboard. "Do you think she is?"

"What?"

"Do you think Aunt Fish is real?"

Miller grunted. "Don't know. And it doesn't matter. Do you even know ma's maiden name?"

Jeannie's lip quivered. "I think it might be Slattern or something."

"Yeah, but I ain't never seen it written down. And ma ain't said it for years. I don't even know if that's it for sure."

"She used to talk about the Slatterns. I figured maybe that was her name.

"I remember." Miller twisted his hands on the steering wheel. "What kind of family don't even know their mother's name?"

Jeannie didn't answer. After a time, she pulled her feet up and hugged her arms around her legs. "It's cold in here."

"I know. Don't think about it."

"That don't make it less cold."

"Thinking about it doesn't help." Then he looked at Jeannie. "Is that what Anna Bostwick said they're gonna do? Try'n find our family?"

"No. I don't know."

"Well which is it? No or I don't know?"

Jeannie shrugged.

"What did she say?"

"She asked me a bunch of questions."

"What about?"

"Family and stuff. About who else, besides mamma and daddy."

"What'd you tell her?"

"Wasn't much to tell. Just like we was talking about now."

"About the Slatterns?"

"I guess."

"You think she believed you?"

"Why wouldn't she?"

"A lot of folks don't like people like Anna."

Jeannie cut her eyes over.

"Not because of her as, you know, a person. Because of her job."

"Because folks got things to hide from government people."

Miller sighed. "Yeah."

"Like us." Jeannie blinked slowly. "I wanted Anna to believe me."

Something in Miller tried to soften, but he wouldn't let it. "Why do you think she told you those things? About judges and looking at court records?"

"I don't know."

"To scare you. You heard what she said. They can come back. They have to."

"She seemed like she was trying to be helpful."

"Helpful for what? You want to be given to strangers that don't want us? Ma or pa ain't got no family that we've ever known. If they find any, they'd be strangers."

Jeannie's eyes watered and she wiped them. "Cousin Rebel's a stranger. He scares me."

"We talked about this. We don't want to be here when those men come back."

"Maybe Rebel won't come. We could go somewhere else."

Miller looked up at the darkening sky, then down to the empty road in front of the house. "We can't wait long."

"You could call him. Then we'd know. If he's not coming."

"No."

"Why not?"

"I don't have his number."

"You didn't get it?"

He shook his head. "I don't even know if Rebel has a phone."

Jeannie sniffed. "So there's no way to know if he's coming or not."

Miller didn't have an answer, so he didn't give one. He knew the general direction to Rebel's house—up the north road into the hills—and he thought he could find it. What if the men came back now, while he and Jeannie were still here? How long could he and Jeannie wander aimlessly until they ran out of money?

Then a darker thought crossed his mind. "I forgot the guns."

"The guns?"

"Yeah."

"You're taking the guns?"

"The shotgun and the rifle."

"What for?"

"You know what for. I'll get them."

He was coming around the truck when she rolled down her window and said, "Rebel will have guns."

"I know it."

"Then why—"

Miller stopped and gave Jeannie a hard look.

"Go get them," she said. "I'll make room."

Miller hustled to the house. They'd waited too long. The men looking for pa might come back any time. He'd been foolish to wait for Rebel.

He picked up the shotgun from behind the door, then went to the closet where pa kept the rifle and looked for ammunition. There were a handful of bullets for the rifle and only a couple more shotgun shells. Pa always said if they ever had to use the guns on men, things would be decided with the first couple of shots. They wouldn't need more than that.

Miller didn't see it that way. The shotgun in his hand felt like something more than a tool to shoot a man. He could use it to scare them. He'd need more rounds to do that.

He came out to the truck with the shotgun and the rifle and laid them on top of the things behind the seat and tucked what ammunition they had in with them. Jeannie watched, and when Miller had things packed back into place he said to her, "I want you to go over to the Jacksons."

She stared at him. "What?"

"The Jacksons."

Jeannie didn't move or answer.

"I want you to go over to—"

"I heard you."

"OK, then do it."

"What in the hell for?"

"Just for a little while. I got to go get something."

She looked through the trees to the house next door. "We don't even know them. Daddy don't like 'em."

"It's just for a little while."

Jeannie shook her head.

"The light's on. Mrs. Jackson is there. She's nice. She'll let you in."

"No."

"Just tell her you need to wait with her for a few minutes. Tell her you lost your key and I'll be right back. I will. It won't be long."

"Where are you going? I'll come with you."

Miller was reaching for Jeannie now, trying to get her up and moving. "We're low on shells. And bullets for the rifle. I'm going to get some."

"They won't sell them to you."

"Not with you along." He tried to give her another push.

Jeannie held her ground. "I'll wait in the truck."

"Look, this will go a lot better if you let me do it alone." He didn't want her to know what he would do if they wouldn't sell the bullets and shells to him. He would get them one way or another. "If Rebel's not here when I get back, we'll go on our own."

She looked up. "Go where?"

"Away. Where they can't find us. Until we figure out what to do."

Jeannie stuck her lip out and didn't move.

"Go on."

"I want my bag."

"What?"

"If we're maybe going to Rebel's and maybe we ain't, I want to repack."

"There's hardly room for much. I don't matter what you take, as long as you've got something to wear."

"I want my bag. If we're maybe gonna be sleeping in the truck or something, I want to take some different things."

"Look, it doesn't really matter—"

"You're going to be gone anyway. It won't bother you." She was already pushing Miller away, reaching for her things.

"I don't want you in the house alone while I'm gone."

"I'll hurry. I know what I want to get."

Miller reached for Jeannie, but she pushed him away.

"I'll run out the back if anybody comes. I won't be but a minute."

He sighed. "You better be quick. And you get over to the Jacksons' when you're done."

"I will."

"And if anybody except Rebel comes while I'm gone, you stay over there. Don't let anybody see you. And don't let Mrs. Jackson come out."

"How'm I supposed to do that?"

"You will if you have to. I'll be back as soon as I can."

Jeannie stepped from the truck. "I don't like it."

"I don't either," Miller said. "But we have to."

He wanted to lean over and give her a kiss on the cheek like he used to when they were little kids, but Jeannie had already moved away from him. It would have been awkward and silly anyway.

He watched as she carried her bags back to the house. Then he headed out.

21

MILLER SCANNED the terrain. To the left, the road wound up into the hills. To the right, it twisted and glided down until it reached the riverbed, then turned and paralleled the water.

Miller took the right turn and drove hard. He gunned the straightaways and banked into the curves. When he neared the river, the trees thinned and opened up to flat bottomland. Instead of following the road along the riverbed, he crossed the steel bridge there and headed away from the water toward the state route.

He passed houses and fields. Some cattle roaming in the swampy lowlands. There was a little traffic, then more as he neared the bigger road.

At the entrance to the highway there was a little strip of shops—a gas station with a Wendy's inside, a dirty restaurant with a sign out front that announced Chicken 'N Chops, a closed-down adult store with a broken neon sign showing a woman's legs. On the end of the row was the place he was looking for.

He could have kept going, down the highway until he hit the bigger stores and the Walmart, where what he wanted would be cheaper. But Miller knew his luck would be better here. He pulled into a slot in front of Jim's Guns, and he went inside.

The store was small, but it was packed tight with all manner of guns and munitions. The walls were cinder block, and heavy iron bars hung in front of the two small windows. The front door was glass, but there was another heavier steel door outside that closed at night. Surveillance cameras hung in the corners of the store and outside the door, and two small TV screens bracketed above the back counter showed images from inside and out. Several bright orange signs announced that the building was alarmed and that the cameras sent footage to a separate location.

Miller didn't know if all that the signs said was true, but he guessed it was true enough. The bigger deterrent was knowing that Jim probably had a loaded weapon within reach behind the counter. Even so, the place had been robbed several times.

That didn't stop Jim from keeping shop. Jim was there now, behind the counter where he always was, this time watching an episode of *Bonanza* on another tiny TV screen.

Jim looked up from the TV when Miller came in. Miller didn't waste time. He walked to the counter and pointed to the boxes on the shelves along the wall behind Jim. "Box of twelve gauge and a box of two-seventies."

Jim reached for the boxes and set them on the counter in the little space by the register. "Your dad out in the truck?"

Miller's pa had been bringing him here since he was little, but he'd never come alone before. He shook his head and laid some bills on the counter.

Jim didn't reach for the money. "You know the rules. He's gonna have to come in and pay for these."

Miller left the bills where they lay. "He ain't here."

Jim looked at Miller for a long time.

"I been in here plenty of times when pa bought shells for me. It's the same thing."

Jim's fingers tapped. He looked at the images on the monitors, looked past Miller to the lot in front.

Miller said, "Nobody else is here."

Jim crossed his arms. "That's not the point. You know I could get in trouble, somebody saw you coming out by yourself."

"That's what I told pa when he sent me."

They looked at each other.

"I'll put them in my pocket. Nobody will see. You could say I was just here looking."

"Why ain't your pa here?"

Miller waited. Shrugged his shoulders. Finally he said, "Been drinkin'."

Jim scratched his neck. "I don't doubt it. What's he want them shells for if he's been drinking?"

"I don't ask pa what for when he's into his bottle."

Jim didn't argue.

"I don't bring them shells home, he'll probably come down here on his own."

A hand moved toward the bills. "That wouldn't be good for nobody."

Miller smiled. "Much obliged. You'll save us another trip."

Jim punched some buttons on the register and rang up the sale. He pushed the boxes across the counter. "Put them in your pocket."

Miller did.

"And don't waste any time gettin' out of here. Just get in the truck and go."

"Yes sir."

Miller shoved the boxes deep into his jacket pockets. When he got to the door, Jim called after him. "Tell your daddy hey from me."

Miller waved to oblige, but he didn't turn or slow down.

22

MILLER DROVE back with even greater intensity, picking up speed on the flats so he could use the momentum to keep his pace up the hills, pushing the truck harder than he should into the curves. It was reckless, especially if something would happen or he'd get stopped with the guns and munitions in the truck, but he kept his foot down on the pedal.

A sense of dread was rising in Miller. A feeling that they'd waited too long. That the men would reappear before they could get away. Or that Rebel would arrive and Jeannie would not go with him. Or maybe even that pa would show up, angry and drunk and confused. Or that someone else unexpected would appear, the way there seemed to be a stampede of strangers at the house lately. That he'd miss whatever it was that was coming when it happened. That it was happening right now. That he wouldn't be there to protect Jeannie.

The truck tires squealed into a curve. He knew the feeling of dread was not rational, but that knowledge didn't help him control it.

Miller finally slowed when he came around the last curve before the house. He slowed again once he'd turned off the road onto the drive that went up and split left for his house and right for the Jacksons'. For the first time ever, he took the fork to the right.

He'd been to the Jacksons' house a few times when he was young, always with his ma. It had been a long time ago. He'd never seen his pa talk to either of the neighbors. But old lady Jackson, who he knew as Marylouise, would sometimes wave at Miller and Jeannie or ma from the yard and shout hello. He'd never spoken to Mr. Jackson, only seen him working in the yard or walking from the house to the truck or the truck to the house. Miller was collateral damage. Mr. Jackson didn't like him because of the unspoken grudge he held with Miller's pa. Ma had called it stupid hillbilly pride. Feuding over nothing.

There was movement in the Jacksons' kitchen window when Miller stopped the truck. He got out and crossed the grassy drive. He stopped at the Jacksons' porch, which was lower to the ground than theirs and newly stained. Up close, the Jacksons' place looked much better than his own home did—fresh paint, clean windows, planters and shrubbery around the house. All of the downspouts intact.

He banged the heels of his boots together to try to shake loose what dirt was stuck there, and went up and knocked.

A curtain over the window in the door moved and Mrs. Jackson looked out. Then the door opened halfway and Mrs. Jackson stood in the entry with a puzzled look. "Albert?"

"Yes ma'am. They call me Miller now."

The puzzled look gave way to a flat smile, then something that knitted her brows. "Is everything all right?"

"Yes ma'am. I'm looking for Jeannie."

The brows knitted tighter. "How can I help you?"

"What?"

"How can I help you find your sister?"

He peered around Mrs. Jackson into the house. "Isn't she here?"

Mrs. Jackson opened the door wider so he could see. "No. Why would Jeannie be here?"

She was gesturing him in, but Miller wouldn't go. "She—we were…Jeannie didn't come over here?"

Mrs. Jackson stepped back. "Why don't you come in and sit for a tick?"

It was then that Miller noticed how old she was, older than he remembered. Her hair was gray and the lines in her face were deep. He shook his head. "No. I'm sorry. I thought Jeannie had come here." He twisted abruptly and looked back at his own house.

"You and Jeannie are welcome here any time. Don't let—"

"I'm sorry. I have to go." And he left Mrs. Jackson holding the open door.

Miller sprinted through the stretch of trees toward his house. A dozen steps in he stopped, turned back and ran to the truck. He levered the shotgun out from behind the seat and pushed a shell into the chamber, then pocketed a handful more shells and took off running again.

He stopped a dozen yards short of the house. It was quiet and the door was closed. Miller whistled once for Bailey. The dog didn't come.

He moved slowly up to the house and onto the porch. There was no sound. He called to Jeannie and waited. Looked around the yard, whistled again for Bailey. Waited.

He called for Rebel and waited. Called out for his pa once and listened.

Then he tried the door. It was unlocked. He hung the shotgun down along his leg and reached across with his other hand for the knob.

When he cleared the door, it swung closed behind him and he saw the movement, the man jumping behind him, then he felt the arm chopping down on his right hand and the boom as the shotgun went off.

Miller's ears hurt and the sound reverberated through the house. A hole gaped in the floorboards by his boot. The adrenaline rose in Miller and he tasted rust and grit. He didn't feel pain and his foot was intact.

He'd managed to hold onto the shotgun, and he spun hard and drove the stock into the center of the man who'd hit him.

There was a grunt and a loud rush of air, and the man bent over.

Then another figure appeared on the other side of Miller and he felt the shotgun being wrenched from his grip. He tried to hang on but his arm was twisted backward and the gun came loose, and then it came down on top of Miller's head.

He stayed upright for a second, then blinked and fell to one knee. The sharp tip of a boot buried itself into Miller's ribs, and he folded down and yielded himself into a ball.

More boot tips came at him and Miller tucked his arms over his ribs then at his head to try to block them. His mind was entering a dark place and then one of the men grabbed the other and said, "Take a breath."

"Fucker hit me."

There was another glancing kick and some scuffling. "He ain't hurt you none."

"Take a poke in your pecker and see if it don't hurt."

Another boot tip grazed Miller's ribs, but without much heat in it.

"We warned you, motherfucker."

They had.

One of the men said, "Get up."

Miller's ears felt thick and his head swam, but he got up. He already knew it when he saw that these were the men who'd come before looking for his pa. The men he'd sent on a fool's journey to look for a sawmill that wasn't there in Munson.

The man who had the pistol in his belt the last time held Miller's shotgun now with the barrel toward the floor. He called to the thin man with the bad beard. "Go get him a towel."

"I ain't gettin' nothing."

"I said get him a towel."

Miller heard bootsteps going into the kitchen. Then bad beard came back and flung a towel at Miller. Miller pressed the cloth against his chin, his temple, the top of his head. It came away with blood, but not soaking.

The man holding Miller's shotgun regarded him. "This don't have to be so hard."

"Tell your friend."

The other man raised a hand.

"Virgil!"

"Well goddam. The little shit ain't but trouble."

The man with Miller's gun said, "Remember what we come for." He motioned Miller to the couch. "Sit down."

Miller said, "I don't care to."

"Now you're just makin' this hard again."

Miller knew where things like this went with men like these. He was hurt, but his pa had done worse to him, plenty of times. It was best to look for a way out. He went to the couch and sat.

The men stood in front of him.

Miller said, "Where's my dog?"

"That mutt was here last time? There weren't no dog."

Virgil bad beard laughed. "Were, wouldn't be no more."

That was good. Miller figured Jeannie for hiding in the woods with Bailey. Like he'd said. He brought the towel from his head. "What'd you want?"

"First off," the man with the gun said, "is you need to show some proper respect. It ain't a kind thing you did sending us over to Munson."

Miller sat, trying to work out new lies in his head.

Virgil moved his menacing boots up to Miller's toes. "What you got to say, boy?"

Miller shrugged.

"There ain't no sawmill in Munson, and your daddy ain't working there."

"It's what he said."

Virgil smirked, his misshapen beard twisting the grimace crooked. "Maybe your pa's a liar?"

Miller stared forward.

"Or maybe you are."

Miller said nothing.

"Where's Zebulon?"

"I guess he ain't at a sawmill."

Virgil's boot came up. Miller shifted away and the boot heel came down on the floor.

The man with the gun hooked the thumb on his free hand into a belt loop. "We don't need to do all this. We just want Zebulon."

Miller wondered if it was some kind of good cop, bad cop. But these men didn't seem smart enough for that. "I told you I don't know where pa is. He said he was working over in Munson. He ain't been home since—"

"Shut up."

Miller did.

"Well?"

"You told me to shut up."

"Don't be an ass like your pappy. Where is he?"

"I keep telling you, I don't know."

The man looked around the house. "Where's your ma?"

Miller stayed silent.

"You telling me you don't know where your mamma is, boy?"

Miller didn't say.

"Who's taking care of you?"

Miller looked up. "Hillfolk business is they own."

The two men looked at each other.

Miller said, "Someone heard the shotgun. They'll come."

The man holding the gun said, "Nobody'd even blink around here for a shotgun." He cocked his hip with the thumb tucked in the beltloop. "I heard you call for your pa. Why was that if you don't know where he is?"

"Thought maybe he'd come back. Looks like he ain't."

The man looked over Miller's wounds. "You don't look too terrible bad. You feeling all right?"

Miller nodded.

"That's fine. Then you'll be clear-headed enough to deliver a message to your pa when you see him."

"What's the message?"

"Your daddy's got a debt to pay."

Miller waited.

The man said, "You got that?"

"I got it. What's the debt for?"

The man smirked. "That ain't the message. What you're askin' is between menfolk."

Hell. Miller felt as much a man as these two. He kept his voice in flat, even tones. "Don't come around here no more. My pa's debt ain't passed to me. You can leave me alone."

It was the way men in these hills thought. A man paid his debts or his family was forced to stand in for him. Or be held accountable. Miller had seen that it rarely got people what they wanted.

The man leaned close so that Miller felt his breath. "What'd you say?"

"I said don't come around here no more."

"Boy, it ain't that simple." He leaned back. "Maybe you need some motivation." He nodded once at Virgil.

Virgil raised a boot and crashed it into the lamp beside Miller. The lamp skittered across the room and tumbled and broke.

"Where's your pa?"

"I don't know."

The man nodded to Virgil again. Virgil went to the kitchen and Miller heard cupboard doors rattle and dishes breaking on the floor.

Miller sat still while Virgil crashed the kitchen.

The man spat on the floor in front of Miller. "I didn't say this debt was passed to you. This ain't the kind of debt that can be passed to kin. This here is personal." He twitched his cheek and spat on the floor again. "I said I want to know where your pa is. Ain't nobody here going to find any peace until we do."

That was shit. Miller was of no mind to pay for his pa's sins. Nor let Jeannie.

Virgil came back from the kitchen and said, "I find you been lying to us, I'm gonna come back and kill that dog of yours."

A hot coal lit in the back of Miller's head. If he had the shotgun in his hand he wouldn't have thought hard about using it. "I told you like it is. Pa ain't been here."

The man with the shotgun said, "He will be. Men like him always come crawling home when they're in trouble."

Miller didn't think the man knew his pa very well.

"The sooner you let this happen, the sooner it will be over."

Miller felt that coal in his head smolder. Goddamn hillfolk. These men would take from Miller for something he hadn't done and call it a principle. His ma had been right when she said men here would fight to any length over anything, or even nothing.

The two men turned away.

Miller called out when they reached the door. "Leave me my gun."

They ignored him and walked out into the thickening morning sky.

Miller went to the window and watched as their truck disappeared. He looked at the sky and wondered when the rain would start to fall.

23

MILLER SEARCHED for his sister.

He started in the bedrooms and the closets and the laundry nook. "JEANNIE!"

He maneuvered through the kitchen around the broken plates and bowls. He checked the lean-to and the woodpile, found the mason jar he'd hidden there and the forty dollars still inside it.

He went to the front porch and whistled, called out, "Bailey!" Listened for the crunching of leaves that meant the dog was coming, but did not hear it.

The more he looked, the more he fought a tremble that was working itself into his thoughts and his bones.

Options crashed through his head. Jeannie was in the woods. She hadn't heard him call yet.

Or Rebel had been here. But they wouldn't leave without Miller. Unless maybe the men had come while Rebel was here?

But Rebel would have stood his ground. Unless…?

Or could Anna Bostwick have come back?

One thing cut through and made clear sense. Miller crossed back to the Jacksons' drive and the truck and pulled the Winchester from behind the seat. He drew back the bolt and chambered a round. It went against what he'd been taught, to leave a round one twitch or jerk or quick grab from release. But so many things went against what he knew should be right.

He clicked the safety on and laid the rifle on the truck seat. Turned and whistled again for Bailey. Walked back to the house and climbed into the attic to check his old hiding place with Jeannie when they were kids. The attic was dark and cold and empty. She was nowhere.

When Miller came down, Bailey was in the kitchen working noisily at a bowl of extra food Jeannie had put down for him. Miller went to the dog and bent to lay a hand on his back. "Where's Jeannie?"

But Bailey was only interested in the food. The dog gulped until Miller took the bowl away and set it on the counter. He swept a path with his foot through the broken plates and bowls.

Then Miller went to the porch and called out again. "Jeannie!"

He lowered his head and listened. Ignored the pain on his scalp and in his ribs.

Miller heard motion in the leaves around the corner of the house. The air went out of his lungs. He'd been a fool to leave the rifle in the truck.

The sound came again and Miller caught the motion of a squirrel moving through the leaves, then the scamper of Bailey coming around from his dog door. Miller whistled to Bailey, but the dog stayed with the squirrel.

He knew then. Miller knew that Jeannie had not run off into the woods. He knew that Rebel had never been here to get her.

He lifted his eyes to the cloud-covered sky. Jeannie hadn't gone to Mrs. Jackson's. The men who were looking for his pa had never seen her. Jeannie had gone off before the men got here.

But with who?

His mind worked through the possibilities.

He saw curtains move in the window next door. But Mrs. Jackson wasn't looking at Miller. She was looking down to the road.

Miller looked too, and far down the road he saw a car coming. He recognized something about the shape of it. Lights on top.

He was in the truck and had backed around in the weeds and was on the road before the county car reached the drive. They passed going opposite directions, Miller's head down as the car swept by.

Then he was heading north, up into the hills. Away.

Away from the police car and Mrs. Jackson. Away from the house and Bailey. His ancestral home. Away from Rebel and the men and his father's debt. Away from everything.

To find what was lost.

His vision sharpened and his hands gripped more firmly on the wheel.

Miller was alone.

PART 2

24

MILLER DROVE.

Rain fell in a mist so fine it was almost a fog. A ghost rain. Over time it clouded the windshield until Miller couldn't see, and he wiped it away.

The road came back into view, but Miller's thoughts stayed in the fog. Images came back to him that he thought he'd pushed away. The dead men. The shovel flashing and digging into flesh. The gunshot and the blossom of red. Dragging the bodies into the men's truck to get rid of them.

The look on Jeannie's face as she helped him.

He swiped the windshield again and tried to wash the images away, but they wouldn't go.

The hills and twisted road grew slick.

Miller drove. He swiped. His thoughts pulled him to dark places.

Eventually, one thought rose above the others.

Where. The hell. Was Jeannie?

That led him to a single thing. A phone. His phone, in Jeannie's pocket. Could he remember the number?

On a narrow shoulder at the top of a brushy curve, Miller turned the truck around. His eye went to the gas gauge and he calculated how much farther it would drop as he drove to town.

He slowed the pace to save gas. Pushed the stick into neutral on the down grades and caught the upslope with enough speed to jam the stick into high gear.

It kept him busy, but the mist swept endlessly at him and brought with it mirages floating on the wind. Blood on the shovel. The blade cutting into neck. The look on the man's face when he knew what Miller had done to him.

Jeannie struggling against the man who tried to pull her into the woods. The gun. The crunch of the leaves under their feet as they dragged the bodies.

The red burbling from the man's chest as he lay on the ground. The wheeze of air escaping from his chest. The red spreading, the garbled breath slowing.

Jeannie.

The dead men's faces. He knew he'd had to do it. But they would not let him go, the dead men inhabiting his head.

It was a relief to exit the tunneled drive beneath the trees and enter the little town. Miller's mind cleared and focused as he parked outside the market.

When he walked in, Miller's nose took him directly to the food donation barrel. He was already hungry.

A half-dozen people working or shopping were scattered near the front of the store by the deli and the check-out. Miller pretended to ignore them while he waited for a chance to reach into the barrel unseen.

He would look for cans. Spaghetti or chili mac, something with a pop top that he could eat with his fingers.

He heard the whispers when his hand was down in the barrel.

Don't they make them go to school?

I'm not surprised. You know how Zeb and Mira raised those kids.

Wheels clicked in Miller's head. Who was watching him reach into the food barrel?

It was Friday. He was going to school. But not for what they thought. He worked on a story. And how many cans he could carry.

Zeb must'a done that to him. You know he's beat that boy like a dog since the day he came into this world.

Miller dropped the cans and his hand went to his face. He felt the aching spots, and heat rose in his cheeks. Then something solidified in his mind and he felt a resolve.

He straightened. Miller turned to the voices and saw Dylan Mott's mother and another woman he didn't know. Miller said, "My mother asked me to pick up some cans of food for the shut-ins at the church. It counts as service time toward my graduation requirement."

Both women stiffened in place.

Miller reached back into the food barrel and turned cans to find what he wanted. "I got kicked by a gelding over to Harson's when I was cleaning a stall. It's healing up all right."

The women both looked down.

Miller was ashamed how easily the lies came. How much he wanted the women to accept them.

He took the cans to the counter and set them in front of Bud who always worked the checkout. Bud nodded at the cans as if he wondered why they were there. "Items from the food barrel are free."

Miller nodded. "Much obliged. I'll need some quarters if you can spare them."

Bud's eyes drifted over the marks on Miller's jaw. "How many?"

"Two dollar's worth?"

"I can do that for you." He reached into the till and counted out coins.

When the trade was done, Miller tucked the coins into this pocket and the cans under his arm.

Bud looked Miller in the eye and didn't give so much as a glance to Ms. Mott and the other woman, who were still watching. When the metal bell hanging at the top of the door jangled as Miller walked out, Bud called after him. "Now say hi to your ma for me."

Miller let the door go. "I will."

He got in the truck and circled the dollar store to the gravelly patch behind where the delivery trucks parked. It was scant relief from windows and prying eyes that belonged to folks with too much time and not enough inclination how to spend it.

Miller popped the top on a can of chili mac and dug in with the fat blade of his pocketknife. The food was gelatinous but warmed and softened as he chewed. Even this was a welcome relief from being his own cook. He finished the can and wondered guiltily what Jeannie had to eat.

Miller put that thought aside and drove to the edge of town.

The school sat hunched back from the road across a patchy stretch of wet bottomland. The grounds clung to the side of the river. The squat building held all thirteen grades in two wings, left and right.

Miller threaded the truck into a little klatch of houses across the road from the school. The dozen or so homes made a boxy grid connected by roads that were more broken and potholed than paved. He parked at the dead end where the road petered out to a walking path that led into the trees.

Miller considered the rifle. He opened the chamber, removed the round, and fed that back into the magazine. He left the chamber empty and checked that the safety was on, then tucked the gun behind the seat. He locked the truck doors and hoped to hell the gun would still be there when he returned.

The rain was holding off, but dark clouds clung to the hilltops and draped down the slopes in cold, gray ribbons. Miller zipped his jacket and pulled the hood up, then he slipped across the road and the wet grass toward the wing on the right that held the upper division.

A high and rusting chain-link fence surrounded the football field. He toed the links, climbed, and dropped to the hard-packed ground on the inside. He walked with the aluminum stands between him and the building and its windows.

When he reached the entry by the athletic offices, Miller walked quickly like he had somewhere to go. Past the open gym doors and a class playing volleyball. Avoiding the main hallway where anyone moving would draw suspicion. Bypassing the principal's office, which he had never gone to when Mr. Ellsburg sent him there the last time he was here.

He crossed the gym lobby to the payphone and dropped in his quarters. Squinted, thought about the numbers, and dialed.

"Biscuit Heaven."

The voice was loud. Miller held a hand over his ear and the receiver.

"Jeannie?"

"This is Aralees's Biscuit Heaven."

"Biscuit Heaven?"

"Can I help you with something? You want a carryout order?"

"No. This isn't Jeannie Brenning's number?"

"Jeannie Brenning? No."

Miller asked him what number he had dialed.

The man at Biscuit Heaven told him.

Miller said he had the wrong number and hung up. Two quarters down. He switched two digits of the number in his head and tried again.

It rang until a strange voice came on and asked him to leave a message.

"Jeannie, if this is you…" He didn't know how to finish. What number could he ask her to call back?

"Jeannie, don't—"

He hung up.

Miller fingered the remaining quarters in his pocket. He imagined numbers in his head, transposed, and dialed again.

The number was out of service. He didn't get his quarters back.

There were two quarters left. One call. Miller rubbed his palms into his eye sockets, tried to see the number. Knowing

Jeannie should be in school and shouldn't answer. Knowing she almost surely wasn't in school.

The coins were in his hand when he heard someone call. "Are you supposed to be there?"

He looked up. A teacher he'd had last year for American history was coming across the lobby, quick.

"Brenning?"

Miller ducked his head.

Another call rang out. Closer, more insistent. "Mr. Brenning."

Miller turned and ran into the wing. He sprinted past the classroom doors and the voice gave chase but fell away behind him.

At the main office he executed a fast and slippery turn on the slick tiles. A head popped up behind the bank of office windows. A door opened.

Miller ran. He burst out the front doors of the school and veered to his right, legs roiling, circling to get behind the building.

He cleared the structure and heard nothing behind him. Churned into the stringy wooded bramble along the riverbed and ran through that to a curve in the road where the school was out of sight.

There he crossed the road and entered the thicket on the far side. It was an easy walk through scrub trees back to the truck.

Miller got in, checked that the rifle was still there, and drove away without looking back. He'd wanted to look for Rubylee. Maybe find her at lunch, or in the change between classes. Ask her to help him find Jeannie. Ask her if she'd heard from Jeannie. Ask her anything that might help. He just wanted someone to help him.

But that was behind him now. He drove home, watching the gas gauge drift slowly down toward the peg.

Miller coasted down the last curve before the flat where his house stood. When he saw the county car parked halfway up the drive, he palmed the truck back into gear.

The gas needle drifted down. He would have to spend money for gas. After that, he was going to look for Rebel.

25

MILLER FIDGETED. It killed him to drive down to the flats by the river crossing for gas. The extra miles burned up gas both ways, but he couldn't bring himself to go back into town again.

Miller pumped in three dollars' worth, thought about what was to come, and pumped three more. That would be cutting it close. He had to go in twice and ask the attendant to stop the pump at three. The smirk he got both times didn't mean a thing.

Then Miller set his sights on a twisted and rutted path up through the hills that was less a road than it was a memory of something that was once suitable for carrying a vehicle.

The lane cut a jagged scar that was much like the paths the white settlers had cut into these lands in search of ore and coal. Miller wondered as he took the truck slowly up the dirt and gravel road if this had once been an ore trail, carved by carts laden with what could be taken from these hills.

He passed by side cuts too rutted or washed out even for the truck to navigate, and the fragile dirt and gravel berms crumbled here and there as he went higher into the hills.

Miller knew the way to Rebel's passed through a narrow gap, and he kept his eyes on the terrain looking for what might reveal the right path to turn on.

At a steep switchback that curved around a rock facing, Miller found what he was looking for—a passable track of dirt road that threaded between two rocky ridges.

It was a short distance before his memory jogged at the sight of the cabin on the ridge. Something came back to him from when his pa had brought him here when he was young. Something that had scared him. A movement in the woods.

The memory clarified. Rebel's dogs.

He stopped the truck and the memory became more than a memory when a big shepherd and a mixed-breed hound with wide shoulders emerged from behind the house. The dogs moved quickly toward the truck, the hound lumbering with its nose close to the ground. The shepherd reached him first and put its front paws against the window and looked in at Miller.

The window was up but cracked against the humidity from the mist and rain. The shepherd stretched its nose to the opening and pawed against the glass. The paws raked and the dogs whined.

Miller sighed. He liked dogs, but he knew what they were for up in these hills. Companionship, but also first alert and security. If he was wrong and this wasn't Rebel's place, or if Rebel had moved on and someone else lived here now, that someone might already be drawing a bead on him.

He reached behind the seat for the rifle, set it on the bench seat beside him, and waited.

No one came.

The dogs stayed a long time before they lost interest. The hound left first, sniffing and scrounging in the leaves and duff. The shepherd eventually followed, and the two dogs moved erratically away together down a slope behind the house.

Miller waited a bit longer, then reached for two of the cans he'd taken from the food barrel and slipped out of the truck with the rifle slung over his shoulder by its strap.

He knew now that Rebel must still live there. Images tucked deep in his memory clicked with the shapes and shadows of the house, the ancient smoker on the porch, the fire pit in the yard, an empty clothes line strung between trees.

He called. "Hello the house."

No one answered. The dogs didn't come.

He called again and waited. When he felt he was alone, Miller stepped onto the porch and looked in a window. It was instantly familiar. The small living room and the kitchen behind it. A single bedroom to one side.

He turned his gaze across the dirt road he'd come in on and remembered. The path up the hill into the trees. His feet took him there.

The dogs found him again when he reached the road. They came from the trees ahead and bounded toward him. Miller stood ready with the cans. He popped a top and threw the can hard. It spiraled and landed up the road between him and the dogs.

The shepherd reached the can first, licking and pawing at the lip to get the food out.

The hound fought the shepherd for a moment, trying to get space at the mouth of the can. It gave up and looked down the road to Miller.

Miller tossed the other can. The hound pounced on the can, and Miller scrambled up the wet slope on the path into the trees.

Branches dripped water from the rains as he brushed by them. Fifty yards in, Miller found what he'd hoped would still be there. The old shack.

The shack was a large lean-to that had been enclosed with plywood and two-by-fours. It made a tight little rectangle with a narrow door on one end and a stovepipe rising through the roof on the other. Inside had been one thing: his pa's still.

Miller checked the rusted lock on the door and found the hasp hanging loose, its screws swelling away from the shrunken and rotting door. He unfolded a blade from his pocketknife and worked the tip behind the hasp at the holes that held the screws. With a few swipes the hasp fell away and took the lock with it.

Miller stepped inside. Everything was as he remembered. As if his pa had simply walked away one day and no one had ever come back. The only other intruder was a thick layer of dust that had blown in through the cracks.

Miller ran a hand over the copper vats and let it spiral down the cooling coil. Touched a finger to the ashy remains in the pit below the boiler.

He inspected musty boxes stacked on a counter that ran

along the back wall. Inside he found empty bottles and more dust. The tattered remains of a fifty-pound bag of sugar littered the floor. A saccharometer rested on the lip of a fermenting barrel. He wondered how many ants had swarmed the place in warmer weather.

Miller looked into the scant cupboards and searched behind the barrels and vats. There was no sign of even a drop of whiskey anywhere.

His thoughts turned to Rebel and the house, but the ghostly presence of his pa teased him and rooted him in the shack. He imagined the smell of the mash as his pa poured it from the barrels into the boiler. The heat from the fire as the still warmed up. The drip of the liquor as it passed from the condensing line.

The ghost of his pa was strong in this place. Miller didn't know why, but it kept him lingering there.

26

MILLER KNEW he'd dozed. What he didn't know was if the sound in his head came from his dreams or outside the shack.

He listened and the sound came again.

It was an intermittent scuffling of leaves. It came, went, and came again. Miller's eyes went to the door that hung open by the width of a boot or more. He hadn't locked the dogs out.

His fingers remembered the rifle in his hands and his grip tightened around the stock. A slanted shadow flickered across the open space in the doorway.

Miller slowly and carefully pulled his feet under him and lifted onto his toes. His fingers felt along the rifle and rested on the bolt.

The door swayed open.

Miller slid the bolt back and a round slipped into the chamber.

The toes of a heavy black boot appeared from behind the edge of the door.

Miller let out a breath. "Rebel?"

The boot came up and pushed the door open. "Boy?"

Miller lowered the rifle.

Rebel spilled into the open door frame, a shotgun leveled at his waist. His eyes cut roughly around the shack and then settled on Miller. "Damn, boy, I could'a blowed your head off."

Miller rolled back off his toes. "I know it. Me too."

The hasp from the door dangled from the fingers of one of Rebel's hands. He dropped the hasp and lowered the shotgun. "What're you doin' up here?"

Miller shrugged. "Where were you?"

"Where was I when?"

"You were supposed to come and get us."

"Get you?"

"Me and Jeannie, at the house."

Rebel dug some fingers into his hair. "I said that, didn't I?"

"You did."

Rebel crossed the shack to Miller. "I was out looking for some men I thought might'a knowed something about your pa. I plum forgot you."

Miller laid the rifle across his folded legs. "Jeannie's gone."

"Gone? Where?"

He shook his head.

"Damn, boy, what d'you mean she's gone? Where could she have gone to?"

Miller's eyes said he didn't know. "Those men came back. And a woman."

Rebel jerked the shotgun up as if by instinct. "They what? What woman did they bring with them?"

Miller was shaking his head. "No. The woman came separate."

Rebel squatted and set the shotgun carefully on the dirt floor. Then he sat next to Miller. Rebel smelled of cigarettes and must and something like old leaves. Over all of that, the smell of a big man who sweated. He said, "You best tell me what's going on."

Miller started with Anna Bostwick. Rebel listened to the whole thing and then made a decision. "The county doesn't have Jeannie. Them people don't move that fast."

"Jeannie took her card."

"What card?"

"The woman's. Anna."

Rebel tilted his head at Miller.

"She told us to call her Anna."

"I didn't say anything about it."

"I think Jeannie liked her."

"The woman with the Child Services?"

Miller didn't like the way it sounded from Rebel, him and Jeannie being children that had to be taken care of. But he guessed that was the way it looked, and the way it was.

"You think Jeannie would call her?" Rebel said. "The county woman?"

"I don't know."

"You have her number? Can you call her?"

"No."

"What about Jeannie? Can you call her?"

Miller told him about going to the school and trying to remember the number to call his phone that Jeannie had.

Rebel pinched the bridge of his nose. "Damn, Miller."

Miller's eyes went up. At least Rebel hadn't called him boy again.

"What about the men? You saw them at the house?"

"They come in."

Rebel dug his fingers into his hair again. "While you were there?"

Miller told him.

Rebel listened, his head swinging no the whole time. When Miller was through, Rebel's head stopped swinging and his jaw set tight. "Shitfire. This is fucked."

Miller knew it was.

"And they said your pa had this debt to them? But they didn't explain it?"

"They said it was personal."

Rebel pulled a hand over his face. "That ain't good. If it was just money, there might be something more we could do about it. But this thing, the way they're telling it...and knowing Zeb."

Miller shifted on his haunches.

Rebel nodded to the marks on Miller's jaw. "And they did that to you?"

Miller's face warmed. "I gave some back to them."

"I guess you did. That help you any?"

"No."

Rebel seemed to approve anyway. He worked his hairline again. "That thing about your pa having a debt."

Miller waited for more.

"I heard some folks talking. Said Zeb looked scared. Does that sound like your pa?"

"Pa's too mean to be scared."

"That's what I mean. You ever seen your pa afraid of anything?"

"Not that he would show it."

Rebel gave Miller a long look. "I guess that's about right."

Miller's fingers twitched on the rifle. He thought of the round in the chamber. Should he back it out? Was he more safe with an empty chamber or a gun ready to use? It was hillfolk thinking, he knew, and the fact that he couldn't come up with a decision bothered him. He looked over to Rebel. "So what's that all mean?"

Rebel pawed at the tufts of hair he'd been pulling, trying to flatten them. "I'd like to figure that out." He stood and brushed the seat of his pants. "I've got to find them."

"Find who?"

"Them people who've been talking about your pa."

"What about Jeannie?"

"She's probably with a friend."

Miller's mind went to Dundee Slocum and Rubylee, but he didn't tell Rebel about them.

"You left her alone," Rebel said. "What was she supposed to do?" Miller winced at the harshness of it, and because he knew Rebel was right.

"I don't think those men have her. They did, they'd have let you know it."

Miller didn't disagree.

"And if the county has her, she'll be safe enough until we can do something about that."

Miller didn't know about that. He liked Anna, but government people didn't sit right with him.

"And if Jeannie's hid herself, let her stay hid. That'd be the best thing for her."

"I don't like it."

"There's nothing to like about it. But that's the way things are." Rebel bent to pick up the shotgun. "I'm going out to look for somebody who knows something."

Miller rose. "I'm coming with you."

"No you're not. This ain't going to be pretty. You stay here and the dogs'll keep you safe. Or let you know to run."

"Those dogs don't like me."

Rebel put a finger and thumb into his mouth and whistled once, high and keening. "They'll like you if I tell them to."

He whistled again and a moment later the dogs came running, the sound of them trampling through the leaves growing nearer. The shepherd burst through the open door of the shack and staked territory beside Rebel. The hound followed.

Both dogs barked and whined, but Rebel held a hand to them. He walked to Miller and clapped him on the shoulder. The dogs knew. The shepherd put its head down and pushed it between Rebel and Miller.

Miller let it happen. The dogs settled and Rebel stepped back.

Miller pushed the dogs aside and straightened up. "I'm coming with you."

Rebel grinned. "You're Zeb's son, all right."

Miller guessed he was.

"You think that old truck you come in will make it down the hill? You can follow me?"

Miller instinctively reached for his pocket with the key.

Rebel was ready. He grabbed Miller's arm and pulled it away from the pocket. Then he stepped behind Miller to pin the arm.

The pain was sharp. Rebel reached around into Miller's pocket and had his keys out before Miller could think. Then Rebel let Miller's arm go and stepped back to thumb through the ring. Miller let him. He had no way to stop Rebel.

There were two keys, one for the house and one for the truck. Rebel identified the truck key and twisted it free from the ring.

He tossed the other key back to Miller. "I'm sorry it had to be like this. Don't take it too hard."

Miller squared his eyes on Rebel. "I won't."

"It's for your own good. Door to the house is unlocked. You can go in and get warm."

Miller said nothing.

"Anybody finds you here, you use that gun and do what you have to."

Miller did not speak or blink.

Rebel turned away. "I'm sorry, boy." He walked away and the dogs followed him.

27

MILLER LISTENED.

Some minutes passed. He thought he heard the muffled clink of a truck door closing in the distance, then the muted drone of an engine.

Miller stepped from the shack. No dogs came. He scrambled down the wet and overgrown path to the dirt road and caught sight of a truck tailgate disappearing downslope.

He ran to his truck, bent behind the driver's door, and put his shoulder to the ground. He leaned under the side panel and his fingers worked up and over the rusty frame rail and ran along the channel until they closed on a small magnetic key safe.

The metal box was rusted, and the key inside was tarnished. But the engine ignited when he put the key in and turned.

Miller gave chase.

Two turns into the descent, Miller braked and the truck slowed and skittered on a wet patch of weeds crowding in from the berm. He cranked the wheel against the steep drop off the side of the road. The truck came back but juddered sideways and the rear tires sank and spun.

Miller opened the truck door and looked back. The tires were slick with muck and mired in a mudded rut.

He let the clutch out in low gear and the tires spun. Mud flew in jets behind the wheels.

He pushed the truck into reverse. The tires dug deeper and inched the frame down into the rut.

He moved the stick into second and slipped the clutch, holding pressure halfway through the release and giving the tires just a taste of torque. The tires spun and he fast-clutched into third and gunned it.

The truck struggled, sighed, and remained stuck. Miller got out to look.

It took him a few minutes to wrestle up the planks that lined the bottom of the truck bed. His pa had put them there to cover the holes that had rusted through. Miller sometimes used the planks to push a wheelbarrow loaded with firewood up into the truck.

Now he used them under the tires, wedging the ends under the rubber treads. He wedged planks behind the tires and shoved a second row underneath the edges of the first, stretching the last planks back onto higher ground.

He got back in and the truck slipped and groaned out of the pit.

Miller retrieved the muddy planks and tossed them helter-skelter into the truck bed. He grinned. His pa would have raised a fit over the haphazard mess. Miller left it like it was.

He righted the truck and pointed it down the wet dirt road, but his heart had gone out of the chase. Rebel would have reached the bottomland and the paved road there, and he'd be long gone before Miller could get off the hill. He backed carefully around and took the truck back up the hill.

When he got to Rebel's cabin, the dogs were still gone. Miller climbed onto the porch and let himself into the house.

He checked that no one was there. Then he went to the kitchen and looked into the fridge. There was half a pack of hot dogs and a block of cheese. Some eggs and butter and bread, and half a dozen tallboys of Steel Reserve beer. Scattered between them were several sealed plastic containers with things inside that sloshed when Miller shook them.

He left the containers and took out the block of cheese and the bread. He found a paring knife in the drawer and made sandwiches with the bread and cheese.

Miller tucked two sandwiches into his jacket pocket and took one to eat as he wandered the house. He wasn't looking for anything, but as his eyes roved over the shelves along the living room wall it came to him what to search for. He looked closer and found an old hardcover bible.

Miller looked inside the bible's front cover, and there written in pencil in a careful hand were names and dates. Just like his ma had done. Family names, birth dates, marriages, children, deaths. He guessed the name and date at the top belonged to Rebel, and that this was Rebel's birth bible. The bible bought when he was born and handed to him when he was old enough to keep it safe. Where he should keep a record of important dates and events. His wedding and his children's names. Their spouses and children.

If that was true, Rebel's given name was Ezekiel, and he hadn't had much to record. That didn't matter. Miller flipped through the pages looking for what he wanted.

Just like Miller's ma, Rebel had tucked some money between the pages. Miller pulled the bills free without reading what passages they marked.

He pocketed three twenties, all that the bible held. Then he searched the place for a gun and ammunition, or some sort of weapon.

Rebel's hunting rifle was hung by the back door on a strap, but Miller already had his rifle in hand and he left Rebel's there. Nothing else useful turned up. Either Rebel hid them well, or he'd taken the shotgun and whatever else he had with him down the hill.

When Miller was satisfied that there was nothing else in the little house that would be of immediate use to him, he returned to the kitchen and found sleeves of crackers and a jar of peanut butter in the cupboard. He pocketed those and reached into the fridge for a couple of the tallboys. He didn't know if he'd drink them, but he wanted them anyway.

Miller locked the front door and went out the back and left that unlocked. Then he drove carefully down the hill, thinking about eating another of the cheese sandwiches. He concentrated on the road and left the sandwiches tucked into the glove box.

He drove into town and to the gas station. He planned to put one of the twenties into the gas tank, but he stopped instead at seventeen and spent the other three on a box of the cupcakes that Jeannie liked. He hoped it would bring him luck.

28

MILLER LET the truck take him home. He didn't think about why he was going there. He just drove. It was dusk when he arrived.

No one was waiting for him. Not a county car with Anna Bostwick or someone else inside who would try to take him away.

No truck with men who believed his pa owed them something. Men who would take what they believed was owed to them any way they could get it.

No one next door at the Jacksons' looking out the window or through the door to see Miller come home.

No one was waiting on the front porch, and no lights were on in the house. If Jeannie was inside, she was hiding in the dark. He didn't believe the men would break into the house and wait in the cold and the dark. They weren't the kind of men to hide. Or to wait.

He honked the horn once and listened.

Nothing happened. No lights. No Jeannie.

Miller took the truck slowly around the house, through the side yard, past the chopping block and the lean-to with the firewood stacked inside, around the garden plot, and to the old pole barn tucked at the back of the lot where the land dropped off.

Bailey came from around the house and ran in excited circles until Miller stepped out of the truck. Miller patted Bailey's head and looked back at the house. It was still dark with no movement.

Bailey sniffed at the pocket of Miller's jacket where he'd stuffed the cheese sandwiches. Miller knew that if Jeannie were here she would want him to give some sandwich to Bailey. But Miller thought of the extra bowls of dog food Jeannie had set out, and how much he had thought of food lately. He kept the sandwiches in his pocket.

Bailey gave up on Miller's pocket and ran off into the dusk after something. Miller turned to the barn. It was small and weathered, old and leaning to one side in the back. He went inside and pushed some things out of the way. The wheelbarrow, a pile of old lumber, a few rusted lawn tools.

When he'd made room, he backed the truck carefully inside and pulled the big wooden doors closed.

Bailey came out of the shadows and found Miller as he reached the back door. Miller went up the steps and reached for the door. It slipped open before he turned the knob.

He thought of the rifle. Locked in the truck, in the barn. He stepped back.

The door creaked open.

He toppled off the steps into the yard.

The back light came on and blazed into his eyes, and a voice called out.

"Miller."

He put a hand in front of his eyes and looked up. "Rubylee?"

She turned the outside light off. "What are you doing?"

Miller straightened. "What are *you* doing?"

"I'm opening the door for you."

"I don't need you to open the door."

"I'm just trying to be nice." She watched him get up. "Did I scare you?"

"No."

"You looked scared."

"I wasn't scared. I was just surprised."

"Well it looked liked scared to me."

Miller came up the steps again and through the door. "It wasn't. Why are you here?"

Rubylee held the door open for Bailey. "I came looking for Jeannie."

Miller frowned. "Why would you do that?"

"I know she's gone."

He gave her a hard look. "How'd you figure that?"

"She's not answering her phone. And Dundee's gone too."

Miller thought about it. "What d'you mean he's gone too?"

"Same as Jeannie."

"Dundee's not answering his phone?"

"My brother doesn't have a phone."

"Then how do you know he's gone?"

Rubylee didn't answer. He guessed she thought it was too simple to explain. "How long?"

She shrugged. "He was on the bus this morning. I let him talk to Jeannie."

Miller's eyebrows went up.

"She called me. I let her talk to him."

Miller roughed out the timing. When he and Jeannie were waiting for Rebel. Before Anna Bostwick had come. Maybe when Jeannie was alone packing her things. And she hadn't told him she'd talked to Dundee.

"How come your brother doesn't have a phone?"

"It's broken. He dropped it."

Miller let out a long breath. "You think Jeannie and Dundee could be together?"

"Do you?"

He did. "Where d'you think they might've gone off to?"

Rubylee wrinkled her nose. "Nobody tells me anything."

Miller took a long look at Rubylee. He'd never thought much about her before, but he saw something new now. A thing that he'd been seeing in his sister. A girl, but a girl getting old enough to start seeing the world differently than when she was younger. More clearly. Even in the insular world of these hills, there was growing up to do when the time came.

Miller said, "Did you hear the horn when I came up?"

She nodded.

"Why didn't you come out and wave?"

She shrugged.

"I see you let yourself in all right."

"The back door was unlocked."

He reached to lock it now. "I guess it was." Then he looked at Rubylee again. Thirteen or fourteen, with a thin nose and hair that was growing long. Jeans and boots and a worn jacket. A faint spray of freckles fading beneath her eyes. "How'd you get here?"

Rubylee cocked her head. "Same as always. On the bus. When Dundee wasn't there I got off mine and got on yours."

"Huh."

"I've been doing that since grade school."

Miller guessed he hadn't noticed it much, but come to think of it Rubylee had kind of always been there. He started for the kitchen. "We can't stay here."

Rubylee followed him. "Why not?"

Miller didn't answer. He turned on the kitchen light.

"Then why'd you come here if you can't stay?"

The floor was cleaned up. The broken plates were swept up and the kitchen looked clean and as it should. Miller turned to Rubylee. "You cleaned up?"

She shrugged. "Some."

"It was…"

Rubylee hadn't asked. She kept her eyes down. "I know what your pa can be like."

Miller felt something hot in his throat. "It wasn't my pa who made the mess. You know he ain't been home?"

Rubylee took a step back. "Jeannie said. I just figured maybe he'd come back."

"When you saw the mess?"

She didn't answer.

"Well he ain't." Miller opened the cupboard, took out some dog food and filled Bailey's bowl.

Bailey heard and came in from the breezeway and ate.

Miller filled the water bowl.

Rubylee watched him. Then she said again, "Why'd you come here if you can't stay?"

"*We* can't stay." It sounded more harsh than he meant. He tried to soften his voice. "I was hoping to find Jeannie."

Bailey slurped at his bowl. Then headlights filtered through the trees, flickering up from the road below.

Miller cut the light and ran to the back room to cut the light there.

He went to the front window and looked out. The headlights swept past and continued down the road.

Rubylee watched him in the dim light. "What're you doing?"

Miller checked the lock on the door and put the chain on. He turned to Rubylee. "You were sitting here in the dark?"

She crossed her arms and drew her shoulders in.

"Rubylee, did you have the lights on?"

She held up her phone. "I wasn't all in the dark that much."

Miller came closer. "What were you doing with your phone?"

"I was trying to call Jeannie again."

"Again?"

"I've been trying to call her all day."

"What number?"

Rubylee looked confused.

"What's the number?"

She swiped the phone and held the screen up for Miller to see. It was the number he'd been trying to remember. A combination he hadn't tried. "That's my phone."

Rubylee pulled her hand back.

"The number you called. That's my phone."

"It's the one Jeannie's been calling me on."

"I know. Look, what happens when you call?"

"Nothing. It goes to message."

"Like the phone is turned off?"

Rubylee nodded.

Another set of lights dappled the trees and flicked at the windows. Miller froze and listened, watched as the lights moved slowly past and faded. He put a hand on Rubylee's elbow. "We have to go."

She hunched her shoulders like a shiver had come over her. "Now you're starting to scare me."

He took his hand away from Rubylee's elbow. "I didn't mean to. But we have to go. Now."

"Go where?"

Miller was already moving to the back door. "I'll tell you on the way."

29

MILLER LOCKED the door and they left the house to Bailey and drove. Miller didn't plan to tell Rubylee much about what was going on, but it was all aching inside of him and it spilled out.

He told her about Anna Bostwick and the county people that would come and take him and Jeannie away because their ma and pa were gone. When Rubylee didn't say anything, he said, "I know you knew our pa was gone."

He left it hang, and finally Rubylee said, "Jeannie told me your mother was gone too."

"She did? When did she say?"

"Month ago, maybe a little more?"

That was cutting it a little short, but Miller got the picture that Rubylee had known.

"I didn't tell nobody."

Miller looked at her. "I don't suspect you would."

He felt himself relax a little, there in the dark of the truck cab. The heat was on and the rain had stopped for now.

It was quiet, just the headlights out front and the warmth from the heater vents washing over them in the closed space.

The engine thrummed through the floorboards, and Miller shifted easily through the gears as they climbed the hills.

He told Rubylee that some men had come to the house looking for his pa. He left the worst of it out, but he told about Rebel and his promise to come get him and Jeannie, then finding Rebel's place up in the hills and the dogs and his pa's still.

Rubylee listened, quiet beside Miller in the cab. He felt the other thing coiled inside of him, but he didn't tell her what haunted him. The two men he'd killed in the woods with a shovel and the other man's gun. He didn't tell her that Jeannie had been there to see it.

Instead, Miller let a silence settle over them.

After a few minutes, Rubylee said, "Where we going?"

Miller thought about what to tell her. "Did Jeannie say anything?"

"Me and Jeannie talk a lot."

"I mean about where they'd go?"

"Where who would go?"

"Jeannie and Dundee. When they go off together."

Rubylee kept her eyes out on the road like she'd rather be talking about something else. "She won't tell me much about it."

"About her and Dundee?"

"I guess."

"Uh-huh. I assume Dundee's in the truck."

That got Rubylee's attention. "The truck's gone. Daddy said Dundee didn't ask to take it. He's right mad."

"I guess he would be. Does he know that Jeannie is gone too? That she might be with him?"

"Dundee wouldn't tell daddy that."

"Does your pa know that Dundee and Jeannie are… maybe going around together?"

"He don't know. If he did, he'd kill Dundee."

"OK, so it's just us that knows. And if Jeannie is with Dundee, they could be about anywhere."

Rubylee didn't agree or disagree. Miller slowed through a curve when the lights from town appeared ahead. "You know where people go to park?"

"Park?"

"You know, sitting together."

"Just sitting?"

"Lord, I hope so."

"You think that's what they're doing?"

Miller thought Rubylee was playing it dumb, that she knew exactly what he was talking about. "Normally I might think that, but with what all's going on right now I don't know."

"You think Jeannie's a little young for sittin' in a truck with my brother?"

He did, but he knew girls nowadays started sooner than how old Jeannie was. He said, "I think Jeannie is too young for just about everything that's happening to her right now."

It sat between them for a moment. Then Miller said, "Where do you think they'd go?"

"What do you think?"

"I don't know, Rubylee. I was hoping maybe you could tell me something."

Rubylee snuffled.

Miller looked at her. "What?"

"Nothing."

"Did Jeannie ever tell you what they do?"

Rubylee shook her head.

Miller squeezed the wheel and said louder than he'd meant to, "You'd tell me if you knew?"

Rubylee hiccupped something that sounded like a little sob.

Miller felt his body deflate. "Shit. I'm sorry. Don't cry. It ain't like I hit you or anything."

"I ain't cryin'."

"It sounds like you are."

"Then it's not because of you." One more strangled little sob choked up, and Rubylee said, "Mental midget."

Miller was surprised when he laughed. "You learn that from Jeannie?"

Rubylee straightened herself in her seat and shook her head. "Jeannie learned that from me."

He grinned. He did not say doofus, but it almost travelled from his head to his lips. Instead, he said, "So why were you sobbing?"

Rubylee wiped a finger across an eye. "Sometimes girls just do."

Miller knew it was true. Even grown women, in these hills. He'd seen his ma try to hide it.

Rubylee folded her hands across her lap. "It's nothing to do with you."

Miller kept his eyes on the road.

"Sometimes girls just cry. It doesn't mean we're weak."

That he knew. And Miller was coming to understand it even more.

They came into the little town and Miller said, "We need a place to start looking."

They glided past the gas station lights. No one was at the pumps.

Rubylee said, "Behind the school."

"The school?"

"Some of them go there at night. I heard them talking about it."

He didn't ask who Rubylee had heard talking about it. They went to the school and Miller circled around to the back. He drove through the parking lot and behind the dumpsters. They watched the headlights sweep across open spaces. They didn't find anyone.

Then Miller took them across the road to the little plat of streets and they went down each of those and to the dead-end where he'd parked the truck that morning. Jeannie and Dundee weren't there.

They cruised the little town, making a criss-cross pattern of the grid. In fifteen minutes they'd covered most of it and found nothing.

Miller stopped in a dark spot on a side road. Rubylee turned toward him. "What now?"

He was turning it over in his head. He knew where else people parked, where guys had been taking the girls they liked since before his parents' generation. He didn't want to go there.

Rubylee's eyes stayed on Miller as if she expected something. He sighed and said it. "There's one more place."

Rubylee nodded as if she already knew.

He drove them to the woods. Where he and Jeannie had gathered firewood. Where the men had found them. Where he'd done what he couldn't forget.

They bumped along the rutted and washed-out road that cut a twisting path through the growth. The waxing moon threw enough light into the almost-bare trees that Miller began to see shapes and shadows among the trunks. Enough to see a truck if it was parked off the road in the undergrowth.

Miller hoped they'd find Jeannie and Dundee, and no one else. The ghosts of the men he'd killed here gathered in his bones and slowly began to harden him from the inside.

The springs on the truck groaned and tossed them as Miller negotiated the ruts. Rubylee jostled on the bench seat and kept her eyes on the moonlit woods.

When they'd gone the length of the passable road, two or three miles in whole, Miller looped through a small and weedy turnaround and pointed the truck back the way they'd come.

He paused.

Rubylee looked over.

Miller said, "We were probably never really going to find them here." His voice sounded odd to him as it broke the silence that had been settled over them for some time.

Rubylee said, "We had to look. We had to do something."

Miller nodded.

A moment passed. Rubylee said, "You could call the police."

"They'll take us away. The woman I told you about, from the county. She said they'd come back."

Rubylee put two fingers onto Miller's knee.

He looked over.

"I'm sorry."

"For what?"

"I wanted to help you find Jeannie."

"And what about your brother?"

"Dundee'll come home when he wants to. He can. With Jeannie it's different."

Rubylee was right. With Jeannie they didn't know. They didn't even know if she was still with Dundee. Miller shivered at the thought of other options.

Rubylee reached for the knob to turn up the heat.

Miller stopped her. "I'm warm enough."

Her eyes went over him, searching.

Miller turned off the headlights. "You want something to eat?"

"Eat?"

He laid his hands on the steering wheel and looked over to her.

"Now?"

It was a thing to do. Something to break the spell. Release him for a moment from the ghosts and the guilt and the worry. From the dead men, from his lost sister and his family and the men who had come for his pa.

He twisted to reach a hand behind the seat and pulled out the package of cupcakes he'd bought at the gas station. "These were supposed to be for Jeannie. She likes these." He held the package up.

Rubylee seemed confused.

"I was hoping they would bring me luck. Help me find her." He set the cupcakes on the dash. "It's stupid, I know."

Rubylee picked up the package. "It's not stupid." She tore the end open. "Do you have a napkin or something?"

Miller pointed a thumb to the glove box. "In there."

Rubylee dug inside and found a couple of crumpled napkins. She unfolded a napkin and smoothed it, then spread it over her knee. Then Rubylee balanced a cupcake there, and another.

Something loosened in Miller and he took one of the cupcakes from Rubylee's knee and held it up. Rubylee picked up the other cupcake and touched it against Miller's as if in a toast. She said, "Jeannie, if you can hear us, this is for you." She took a bite.

Miller bit too. The soft creamy interior spread through his mouth like the memory of a better time, a better place. He stuffed the rest of the cupcake in and chewed.

Rubylee stuffed her cupcake into her mouth.

Miller reached into his jacket pocket and pulled out the cheese sandwiches he'd made at Rebel's. "Maybe we should eat these too?"

Rubylee nodded.

Miller was suddenly very hungry. He turned off the truck and the cab quieted and the woods around them seemed to lean in closer.

Rubylee unwrapped a sandwich from the paper towel Miller had tucked it into. She placed the sandwich on her knee and tore it in half.

Miller reached behind the seat again and came out with one of the tallboy cans of beer. "I took this from Rebel's house. We don't have to drink any of it if you don't want to."

He expected Rubylee to protest, but instead she took the can from Miller and pulled the top back and said, "I've drank beer before." She took a sip.

Then Rubylee held the can out to Miller and he lifted it for a drink. The beer was cool but not cold. It wasn't enough to hide the bitter taste.

Miller took another drink. He didn't know what he and Rubylee were doing, but he liked the distraction. For a moment he felt freer and lighter.

They ate that cheese sandwich and the other, Miller putting down twice what Rubylee ate but Rubylee mostly keeping up with him on the beer.

When the sandwiches were gone and the beer was getting low, Miller picked up the can, lowered the window, and dumped out what was left.

Rubylee said, "What'd you do that for?"

"I shouldn't have let you drink any. You feeling OK?"

"It's not even a whole beer. I've drunk more than that before."

It hit Miller wrong. What they were doing. He felt guilty about losing Jeannie. About the dead men. About drinking beer with Rubylee, who was maybe fourteen and his sister's friend. And he felt ashamed that everything he and Jeannie had might be taken away.

Miller looked at Rubylee. He knew that other men would see her as old enough, like the men in the woods had seen Jeannie. The shame in him blossomed. He knew women in these hills learned early to try to comfort men, that it was a way for them to survive. He liked Rubylee comforting him, feeding the sandwich to him, holding the can of beer. He liked it but he didn't want to be like those other men.

Miller reached for the key. "I shouldn't have brought you here."

"We were looking for Jeannie and Dundee."

"They're not here." He started the truck. "I'm taking you home."

Rubylee protested most of the way back through the woods. Miller ignored her and kept his focus on the rutted drive.

When they reached the paved road, Rubylee set her jaw and stopped talking. She didn't say a word the rest of the way, even when Miller pulled in front of her house and she got out and left him.

30

MILLER WENT back to Rebel's. He didn't know why he went there, and that didn't bother him. Maybe he thought Rebel would help him find Jeannie, or his pa. Or something else Miller had lost. Mostly he thought he was going back to Rebel's because Rebel felt like a little piece of something that was still solid he could hold on to.

Glimpses of dim light eked out of the darkness down narrow drives as Miller geared the truck up the hill toward Rebel's. He wondered what was at the end of those drives, the few other folks who had carved homes out of the hillsides. Were they loners like Rebel? Or maybe families, with brother and sister like he and Jeannie? Would they greet a stranger at their door with a handshake, or with dogs and a shotgun? Then he wondered the same about Rebel.

When he reached the house, Rebel's truck wasn't there. Miller tried to park in exactly the same spot he had before, inching forward to feel where the tires had dimpled the wet soil.

He opened his door slowly and listened. The dogs weren't there.

He waited, and a moment later he heard them, paws scrabbling through the wet leaves. He stepped out of the truck, ready. Not taking chances. A food-barrel can of pasta and meatballs open in one hand.

The shepherd pulled up in front of Miller, its head lunging for the hand with the can. Miller snapped his hand back and spilled some food onto the ground. The shepherd dove for it, and he tapped what was left in the can out for the hound.

The dogs ignored Miller as he made his way to the house. Halfway there he changed his mind and walked up the dark slope to the shack that held his father's old still.

A little moonlight cut through the clouds and clawed in through the dirty windows. Miller let his eyes adjust and found a slice of firewood from beside the boiler. He wedged the wood between the door and the frame and pushed until the seal tightened.

He knew he should go to the house, get inside and stay warm. He was too tired to think, but his mind was too full to let him sleep.

Miller made a seat of a wooden crate pushed against the wall. He sat and wondered if he could restart his pa's still. The intricacies of the saccharometer were beyond him, but he could get water and sugar and yeast into the barrel and push in the airlocks and get fermentation. He knew that in a week or two the bubbles would slow and he could syphon the mash into the still. And he knew to cook the batch slow at just under boiling, and to throw out the first jar from the drip.

He didn't have his father's steady hand at flavoring, but he could make whiskey, do something to pay off his pa's debt. Even if it wasn't what the men wanted, it was something. And maybe he could make some money for him and Jeannie.

In the dim light and his sleepy state, Miller almost convinced himself he could do it. But he knew when he woke in the morning the task would become impossible. He knew he didn't want to become what his father had been. That he wouldn't accept the legacy that was handed down to him. He would be his own man.

Miller closed his eyes and let that promise wash over him.

Some time passed and Miller knew that he'd been asleep. He was cold and the world was quiet and his thoughts were blank.

He heard a dog whine outside the shack. Then footsteps and the door creaking against the wood he'd wedged there. A slice of moonlight opened with the door and Rebel stepped in. "Boy?"

He was already getting up.

"You should come in the house and get warm."

Miller moved forward. "Give me back my key."

"Your key?"

"The truck key."

Rebel grunted. "That can wait 'til morning."

Miller stepped closer to Rebel. "I said, give me back my key."

Rebel smelled of sweat and dogs. He narrowed his eyes and looked at Miller for a long spell. Then he put a hand into his pocket and said, "I guess you think you're a big boy now."

Miller guessed he did.

Rebel took Miller's palm and pressed the key into it. "Now don't be stupid. Come into the house and get warm."

Miller worked the key back onto his ring. "What'd you find out?"

Rebel's eyes closed and his head swiveled like a pendulum. "What?"

Rebel turned to the slice of light beyond the door. "That—" He kicked the door wide and the dogs were there, whining and scruffling. "Will wait for morning."

Miller followed Rebel down the path to the house and slept on the couch under old blankets, his dreams disturbing his sleep the whole night.

When Miller woke in the morning, the light was gray and rain pattered the roof. The scrape of a chair sounded from the kitchen and he smelled coffee. Miller rose and sat at the little table across from Rebel.

Rebel smoked a cigarette and watched Miller. He stubbed the butt out in a tuna can and pointed to the porcelain coffeepot on the counter. "Get yourself a cup."

Miller opened a cupboard door and found a cup. He filled it with coffee and looked into the fridge. "You have cream? And sugar?"

Rebel laughed. "Damn, boy. It's time you learned to drink your coffee right. Just black will do."

Miller sat across from Rebel again. He took a sip from the black coffee, then another sip. He set the cup down carefully and turned the ear away from his hand. "Black is fine. And my name's not boy. It's Miller."

Rebel grinned. "That what your daddy called you?"

"He called me shit-for-brains."

Rebel cocked his head as if trying to decide if it was true. Then he said, "I'm gonna go with Miller."

Miller gave a quick, tight nod of his chin.

Rebel got up. "You want some breakfast?"

Before Miller could answer, Rebel was pulling eggs from the fridge.

Rebel set a pitted iron skillet on a burner to warm, then dug his thumbs into half a dozen slices of bread to make holes in the centers. He knifed butter into the skillet and browned the bread in it, two slices at a time.

Miller drank coffee and watched. Rebel dropped more butter into the pan, cracked two eggs in, and placed a slice on each egg with the yolk sticking through the hole. "You like gypsy toast?"

"Would'a starved to death by now if I didn't."

When it was ready, Rebel scooped the gypsy toast onto a plate and handed that to Miller. "Company first."

Miller indulged.

He was almost through his plate when Rebel pulled the second batch from the skillet. He ate standing at the counter while he watched the last of the eggs cook.

They split the last two. Rebel had drunk three cups of coffee. Miller sipped one.

Rebel pushed his plate away and belched loudly. "One of the benefits of living alone."

Miller's ma would have said it was a reason Rebel lived alone. His pa would have said "Excuse the pig" and then belched himself.

It was a weird moment for Miller. Sitting there at the little table in the kitchen felt almost like family. But that thought went sour when he realized this might be the closest he would ever come to family again.

Rebel was cleaning his teeth with the edge of a matchbook. He set the matches down and regarded Miller.

Miller said, "You gonna tell me what you found out?"

"I guess I ought to, seeing as how you're Miller now and not just a boy."

Miller didn't find anything to argue with about that, so he waited.

Rebel sucked his teeth and let out a long sigh. "This thing with Zeb is worse than I thought."

"You find him?"

Rebel shook his head. "Nobody has."

"You think pa's dead?"

Rebel looked like he was still deciding what to make of Miller, then he said, "Maybe. Some others think so."

Miller leaned back. He was surprised that he felt betrayed, or something like it. Some kind of grief, maybe. He'd known this might be coming, that his pa might be dead, and he'd thought he was ready for it.

Rebel ignored the look on Miller's face and said, "It might be easier in some ways if your pa is dead."

A little spark lit in the back of Miller's head. "How can you say that about family?"

"Now hang on. I didn't say I wanted Zeb dead. I don't. But if he already is, I'm saying if there's no stopping that, it would put some things to rest."

"What things?"

Rebel worked a finger across the cleft of his chin, thinking again, then he said, "I'm gonna tell you. This isn't about money or payin' off an old moonshine debt."

Miller sat like a stone.

"Be easier if it was. This is about that trouble when your daddy was sellin' shine to them boys running the bars down in the flats."

Miller dipped his head once to show he understood.

"Your daddy and them had a good thing going. But Zeb had a way of fucking up every good thing. When the law came down on your daddy, he ratted some of them others out to save himself. He made a deal and fingered Slake Bowman, and they put Slake into jail."

"Slake?"

"His name was Herbert. I don't know why, but everybody called him Slake."

"Who is Slake Bowman?"

Rebel's lip twitched, then he spat it out. "Everett and Dorsey Bowman's little brother."

Bits of things in Miller's head tried to line themselves up.

Rebel said, "The guys that disappeared."

Miller knew.

"Here about a few days back."

The men who'd come for him and Jeannie in the woods. The men Miller had killed and taken their bodies away.

Rebel pulled a cigarette out of the pack and took his time lighting it.

Miller took his time thinking. "Slake was working with my pa?"

Rebel smoked. "You could say that. Slake was selling your daddy's shine out of his bar. Your daddy turned the authorities on to some other things that Slake was doing illegal."

Miller thought about it.

Rebel looked at the question on Miller's face. "Slake was selling more than just bootleg whiskey."

Miller thought about it some more. "Why now?"

"Why now what?"

Miller shrugged. "Any of it."

Rebel blew away some smoke. "Slake Bowman was supposed to get out of jail last week. He didn't."

"Why not?"

"Somebody shanked him in the prison yard."

Miller let it settle in. "He's dead?"

Rebel nodded.

"That have anything to do with my pa?"

"I don't see how it could."

"Then why…"

Rebel said, "It don't matter. Slake didn't get out, and the Bowmans is pissed. They blame your daddy."

"How's that figure?"

"If your daddy hadn't ratted him, Slake wouldn't'a been in the pokey and got killed there."

"That don't make a lot of sense. Slake got his own self into jail. My pa didn't kill him."

Rebel nodded. "I guess he didn't. But jail's one thing. Dead is different. The Bowman boys see it the way they see it."

Miller guessed they did. "Why'd Slake get killed right before he was gonna get out?"

"That don't matter. Could be just bad timing. Could be someone had a grudge. But it set the Bowmans off. They went out to kill your pa."

Millet let his words out slowly. "You think they did it? They killed pa?"

"Maybe. The Bowmans ain't come home. Maybe your pa killed them."

He didn't. Miller had killed those men. "Then who came to the house looking for pa?"

Rebel sucked on the cigarette butt. "This is where it ain't good."

"The rest of it's good?"

"I guess not." Rebel put a thumb against the edge of the tuna can and pressed a divot into the metal. He laid what was left of his cigarette in the slot. "The men who came to your house are kin to the Bowmans. Virgil and Hank Wilkins."

Miller felt Rebel looking at him as if that should mean something. "Close kin?"

"Cousins."

"Like you and pa."

Rebel nodded. "Close." He watched the cigarette burn but didn't reach for it. "Everett and Dorsey ain't come home. They don't answer their phones. Everett's truck is gone. They disappeared."

"They're not the first men to disappear from these hills."

Rebel picked the cigarette from the tuna can now and drew on it. The tobacco crackled hard. "Virgil and Hank are bad news. They believe your pa killed Everett and Dorsey. Probably when them two tried to kill Zeb. Now the Wilkins want to find Zeb and kill him. For what they think he done to Everett and Dorsey, and to Slake."

"What if pa didn't kill the Bowmans?"

"It doesn't matter with guys like the Wilkins."

It was twisted. Miller's pa hadn't killed the Bowmans, and he hadn't done anything to make Slake sell his bootleg whiskey. But there was some kind of hillbilly code playing out here that couldn't be broken. An eye for an eye, a bible verse for a bible verse. Show you're a man by killing a man who killed one of your clan.

Rebel set the butt of the cigarette into the slot in the tuna can and looked at it as if he was trying to decide if there was anything left worth drawing on. Then his eyes settled back on Miller. "They're not gonna give up. They're not like that. This isn't gonna end until someone's dead. Zeb is going to have to kill Virgil and Hank, or they're gonna kill him."

"Or somebody already did kill pa."

Rebel's eyes dropped. "That's where things aren't entirely clear."

Miller raised an eyebrow.

"Something happened to Everett and Dorsey Bowman. If it wasn't Zeb that done it, then who?"

Miller frowned. "How'd you find all that out about the Bowmans and them other guys?"

"Everybody's talking about the Bowmans and what happened to Slake. The rest…" Rebel tipped his head again as if he was deciding what to tell Miller. "You get to shootin' pool with some good ol' boys who know a little something and let them think they can beat you and take your money, they loosen up a bit."

"You dumped a game of pool?"

"Several. You ever get forty dollars and want to pay me back, I'd be obliged."

Miller put that together in his head with the sixty he'd taken from the bible on the shelf. That made an even hundred. He felt a little guilty, but the guilt was covered up by so many other things it didn't bother him. "So what do we do now?"

"This is all due to your daddy. If he's alive, we've got to find him. And if he isn't, we've got to put this to rest."

"How do we do that?"

"That's what I need to find out."

"We could kill the Wilkins." Miller felt the shame in his words even as they were coming out.

Rebel stared. "Don't even think like that. Things are bad enough." He pushed his chair back and rose.

"Where you going?"

"I'm going to talk to Quirt."

"Quirt?"

"County deputy. Me and him went to school together. Played football together. Normally I wouldn't like talking to no cops, but this is special circumstances."

"What do you want me to do?"

"Do what you want. Don't get shot or killed. Don't do anything that will get me shot or killed. I give you your key back. You can do what you want."

"I want to help."

"You could try and find your sister." Then Rebel tromped across the kitchen floor in his heavy boots and went out the back and let the door swing shut behind him.

Miller pushed his face into his hands and rubbed his palms into his eyes. Goddam hillbillies.

31

MILLER DIDN'T know how in the hell he was supposed to find his sister.

What he did know was that he was tired of driving around in the truck, wasting gas and burning up money. He was tired of the heavy things on his mind, of worry about Jeannie, about the dead men, and his ma and pa. He was tired of losing everything, of what little he had left slipping further and further away.

He was tired of the old truck struggling on the muddy slopes of the steep hill as he drove back down to go to town and try calling Jeannie again. Tired of the weathered and brittle wipers that fought against the rain streaking the windshield. Tired of the fucking rain, which never came down hard but wouldn't let up, just kept coming back at Miller and wearing him down until he felt like he would drown.

He slipped through the last curve in the road before a muddy descent to the paved county route below. There in a straight stretch ahead was a figure walking toward him up the soggy hill. Miller slowed, wondering which of the dim houses above the walker belonged to.

He ground the truck down into second gear and slowed more. The figure walking looked up at him, rain ticking down off the bill of a cap. It was a girl, soaked through in a sweatshirt and jeans. He could see her shivering.

Miller pressed the brake. The truck skidded and stopped, digging into the mud.

The girl raised a hand.

Miller rolled his window down enough to shout through it. "Rubylee?"

She crossed in front of the truck. Miller reached over the seat and cocked the passenger door open. "Get in here."

Rubylee did, squishing into the seat. "Sorry. I'm getting everything wet."

"Don't worry about that. You're freezing." He turned up the heat and the blower. "What are you doing?"

"I came to find you."

"How—I don't even know how you'd get here."

"You told me where it was. I know the roads."

"But how did you even get all the way out here?"

"I rode with a man and woman. Hitchhiked out of the gas station."

"You hitchhiked?"

"I said I did."

"Someone you know?"

"Not hardly. They just stopped for gas."

"That's not a good idea." For Rubylee, or for the man and woman who picked her up. "Who does that anymore?"

"Better'n trying to walk the whole way."

Miller looked at Rubylee hunching inside her wet clothes. "They let you out in the rain?"

She shrugged. "They didn't want to try and drive up the hill. I told them I lived right up the road."

Miller turned the blower up to the last notch. "And you were going to walk up the hill and look for Rebel's?"

"I guess."

"How were you going to find it?"

Rubylee shrugged again. "You told me about it. I was gonna look for the dogs."

Miller shook his head. Everyone had dogs. He leaned the seat forward and reached behind it for his backpack. He dug out his extra pair of pants and his spare sweatshirt and laid them on the dash.

Rubylee was shaking her head.

Miller pulled on his cap and jacket. "I'll be outside." He saw that she was going to protest, but Miller left the truck running and slipped out before she could say anything.

A couple of minutes later Rubylee rolled the window down a crack and said, "Y'all can come back in now."

He did. His cap was wet and his shoes had gotten damp, but he was mostly dry in the middle. Better than Rubylee had fared.

Rubylee said, "You didn't need to get out. It ain't like I don't have a brother."

"I'm not your brother."

She looked him over. "I guess you're not." Then she opened her door and squeezed the wet clothes she'd changed out of. Water ran free, but the clothes were still heavy and wet. Rubylee lowered her window an inch, stuck the waist of her pants into the gap, then cranked the window back up to hold the pants. Then she draped her wet jacket and shirt over the edge of her seat and tilted the blower vent toward them.

Rubylee had the cuffs of Miller's pants and the sleeves of his sweatshirt rolled up. She pulled at the loose waistband. "Everything's too big."

"Of course it is." He reached behind the seat and fished out a roll of twine. He cut a length, doubled that over, and made a belt of it for Rubylee. "Best we can do until your things dry."

She cinched the makeshift belt.

Miller noticed her bare feet. "I don't have any extra shoes."

Rubylee raised her feet and stuck them over the dash vents. "Best we can do."

It was getting steamy in the truck. Miller let his window down a little. "Why'd you come all the way out here looking for me?"

Rubylee picked up her phone from between them on the seat. The screen was wet. She wiped it with the edge of a sleeve. "Jeannie called."

"What? Why didn't you say so?"

"I just did."

"I mean right away."

She frowned. "I tried to. You were standing out in the rain."

"Just tell me what Jeannie said. Where is she?"

Rubylee moved her finger over the phone. "We only talked for a minute. She said to call her back when I found you."

Rubylee dialed. After the second ring, Miller heard Jeannie's voice. "Rubylee?"

Rubylee said, "I'm here. So's your brother." She held the phone out between her and Miller.

Miller leaned in. "Where are you? Where've you been? Where'd you go? Are you OK?"

"Slow down."

"What took you so long to call?"

"Your stupid phone. We didn't know how a minutes phone works. Who does that?"

"Dundee is with you?"

"Yeah. The phone was out of minutes."

"You have to buy more time for it. You can do that at the dollar store."

"I know that now."

"Where are you?"

"Norton."

"What are you doin' way over there?"

"We were sleeping."

"Sleeping?"

"In Dundee's truck."

Miller blinked. He got it. "You never went to Mrs. Jackson's."

Jeannie didn't answer.

Miller said, "They're looking for Dundee."

Rubylee leaned closer. "Daddy's mad."

There was a grunt or some sort of sound from Dundee. Miller said, "What'd you go to Norton for?"

There was a pause that Miller didn't like. Then Jeannie answered. "We went to see Anna."

Miller let out a long breath.

Jeannie said, "That woman from the county who came to the house."

"I know who she is. What'd you want her for?"

"I told her that daddy was gone. And mamma before him."

"What'd you go and do that for? They're gonna come and take us away."

"We're not even there to take away. What're they gonna do?"

"They'll find us."

"She let me go. Me and Dundee."

Miller thought about it. "She just let you walk away?"

"We didn't go to her work. I called her and she told us to go to her house. We talked, and then she let us go."

Miller wondered if there really was trust still left in the world, or if this was another piece of something that would be taken away from him.

"She said she can find mamma."

"Our ma?"

"Yes."

"How's she going to do that?"

"Aunt Fish. I told her about mamma's family."

"Fish ain't her real name."

"I know that."

"Then she'll make us go live with them. They'll take us away."

Jeannie's breath echoed through the connection. "Anna wants to find mamma. She wants us to be with mamma."

Miller didn't even know if that was possible. "Ma's gone."

"You doofus. Can't you let her try to help? Can't you let anybody?"

Miller thought he could hear the tears coming, but Jeannie hung on. He said, "There's some things I've got to tell you."

"Well do it quick. We're already getting low on minutes again."

"It's gonna take more time than that. Let's meet somewhere."

"Where?"

"You hungry?"

There were some muffled sounds, then Jeannie said, "We're starving. We've hardly got any money left. We had to put it in gas."

He knew the feeling. "You know the chicken truck stop place down by the highway?"

"The one daddy used to like to go to?"

"That one."

"Yeah."

"Meet us there."

There was muted talk between Jeannie and Dundee. Then Jeannie came back. "What time? It'll take us a while to get there."

"Just go. Wait if we're not there before you." But Miller knew they would be.

"What about Dundee?"

Dundee's voice came on. "Yeah. What about me?"

"You come too."

That ended the call. Rubylee slipped the phone into a pocket and grinned.

Miller said, "This isn't fun."

"I didn't say it was." But the smirk on her face didn't go away.

32

MILLER SCOOPED mashed potatoes and green beans. Jeannie reached for a chicken leg. "Bible food."

The waitress's eyes roamed their way from across the diner. Miller had told the others about taking the money from Rebel's bible. Now he wished he hadn't.

When they'd come in and sat at one of the booths, the woman had watched them but stayed behind the counter. Miller guessed she was worried they didn't have money to eat, and he'd gone over and shown her the twenties. That had calmed her worries. But it hadn't stilled her roving glances.

Rubylee dug a fork into her food. "Holy mashed potatoes."

One of the truck drivers at the counter cast an eye over. Miller shook his head and said to the table, "You think it's funny?"

Jeannie held a french fry out and wiggled it. "A little. You know the story about the bread and fishes? We got potatoes and chicken."

They wouldn't be laughing when Miller told them what he knew. And that he didn't believe Anna Bostwick would magically find their mother and he and Jeannie would go home and Virgil and Hank Wilkins would go away and life would be good again.

But he let them eat. He let Jeannie have that small comfort while they could afford it.

When Miller had eaten his fill, he picked up the check and crossed the little truck-stop diner to the counter. The trucker who'd looked over before let his eyes wander from under the bill of his cap to Miller as he stood at the check-out.

The waitress decamped from the other end of the counter and came to the register. "Y'all going to need a leftover bag?"

Miller stopped. "No thank you, ma'am. We'll eat it all."

Her eyes flitted to the table and back, and Miller could see that she didn't doubt it. He paid the bill and from the change counted out a tip and pushed it across the counter.

The waitress looked down at the money, then back to Jeannie and Rubylee and Dundee. "That's too much."

He'd done the math. "It's the right amount."

She chewed her bottom lip.

Miller turned. "Thank you ma'am."

He went back to the booth but didn't sit. Instead he stood and looked out the big front window into the gray as the others split one piece of cherry pie between them.

He looked at the hills and tried to see what would come next. What was to come with Rebel, with the Wilkins, with his pa. Where his ma was and why she hadn't come back. What Anna Bostwick and the county people would do, and if he and Jeannie would ever live in their house again. How he would pay for things when the bible money was gone.

He stared for a long time until the waitress's eyes came over again, but more lazily this time. Jeannie forked the last bite of pie and held it up to Miller. "Want it?"

He shook his head no.

"You're kind of a downer."

Miller sat. "I haven't told you yet."

"Told me what?"

He looked at Rubylee and Dundee but spoke to Jeannie. "You want them to hear it too?"

Rubylee said, "Whatever you're gonna say, I already know it."

"You know some of it."

Dundee looked at Jeannie but didn't say anything.

Jeannie said, "You might as well tell. I'd just tell Rubylee, or I'd tell Dundee and he'd tell Rubylee, or Rubylee would—"

"I get it." Miller looked around the table. "Here's what I know."

He told them. He told them that Rebel thought their pa might be dead. He told about Slake Bowman getting killed in jail and the Bowman brothers wanting to kill pa for it. He told about Virgil and Hank Wilkins. Then he sat back and let it sink in.

Jeannie's eyes fixed on Miller. "The men who came to the house…they were there because they think pa killed the Bowman brothers?"

Miller tried to tell Jeannie with a tic of his face not to tell what had happened in the woods. "And for putting Slake into jail, and that getting him killed."

"But they can't know that pa killed the Bowmans."

"No." Miller put up a hand. "I guess nobody knows for sure. But that don't matter. It's what the Wilkins think." He kept his hand up to try to tell Jeannie not to say any more.

Dundee tapped some fingers on the table. The rhythm built then stopped. "It sounds like maybe your pa done it. Done killed the Bowmans."

Miller said nothing. Jeannie watched him and said nothing.

Dundee said, "But if he's dead, how did he kill the Bowmans? And who killed him?"

Miller was beginning to have ideas about that.

Jeannie steered the conversation away and saved him from those thoughts. "What did Rebel say about ma?"

Miller wagged his head. "He doesn't know anything."

"Well, shit."

Miller held a hand out, palm down. "Keep it down." He cut his eyes expectantly to the waitress and the trucker, but they seemed to have lost interest in them.

Jeannie tossed a look toward the counter. "They don't care. You paid her."

Rubylee leaned into the table. "What are y'all gonna do?"

Miller said, "That's a good question." He turned to Jeannie. "Can your Anna Bostwick fix that?"

"She's not my Anna Bostwick."

"You know what I mean."

"No, I don't think I do. Why don't you tell me?"

"You think she's going to fix everything. Find ma. Chase the Wilkins away." Something caught in Miller's throat and he forced it down. "Make pa not be dead."

Jeannie's eyes scrunched up hard and she wiped them. "We don't know if he's dead."

"We don't know if he's not."

It sat there between them, the four of them and the rumpled remains of the chicken and potatoes. What were they going to do?

Jeannie broke the spell by piling chicken bones and dirty napkins onto her plate. She stacked that on top of Dundee's plate. "I want to go home now."

Miller sighed. "So do I." He took his wallet from his pocket and pulled out bills that he extended toward Dundee. "For gas and such."

Dundee shook his head. "You don't need to."

"Take it. I know you don't have much. Jeannie said you were starving."

Dundee's gaze lingered on the bills. "I do need enough gas to get home."

"Take it." Miller wiggled the bills.

Dundee took the money and crumpled it into his pocket. He looked at Jeannie with an apology in his eyes.

Jeannie said, "It's all right."

Miller tucked his wallet back into his pocket. "It won't matter soon anyway. What's left isn't going to last us long." He rose and felt something else rise unexpectedly with him. A decision. A resolve. The answer he'd known but hadn't been able to see. What they had to do. He straightened his back. "It's time for me to get going."

Jeannie looked at him. "Going where?"

"Home. I'm going to take back what's ours."

"How're you gonna do that?"

"Any way I can." He slung his jacket on. "Dundee, you should take Jeannie home with you and Rubylee."

Jeannie popped out of the booth.

Miller already had a hand up, knowing she would protest.

Jeannie did. "You can't go home alone. And you can't make me go away. It's my house too and I—"

"Stop."

"But I—"

"Stop." Another decision came to him. Another thing he'd known but couldn't see. "You're right. It's your house too, and you can come. But you'll have to do what I say."

"I don't want to—"

Miller put a hand on his sister's arm and held it there a long time and looked at her.

Finally, Jeannie's head bobbed and she whispered, "OK."

Rubylee and Dundee climbed out of the booth. Dundee said, "My dad's gonna be real mad."

Miller pulled his keys from his pocket. "You can't run forever."

Dundee scratched his head like he was thinking maybe he could.

Rubylee pulled on the long sleeve of Miller's sweatshirt that hung past her wrist. "I can't go home in these. Wearing some boy's clothes."

Jeannie said, "It's not some boy. It's my brother."

Dundee said, "That makes it worse."

Miller looked out the diner window at the truck and Rubylee's pants dangling from the window. They wouldn't be anywhere near dry yet. He said, "Jeannie, you and Rubylee could change clothes."

Jeannie made a gagging sound. "I don't want to wear your clothes."

Miller still looked out the window. "Is your bag in Dundee's truck?"

Jeannie reddened.

"Is it?"

"Everything's wet. We got in the rain and I had to change."

"Everything?"

"It's all balled up in there."

"Then you'll have to change with Rubylee."

The girls looked at each other. Jeannie said, "They can come home with us. I'll find something for her to wear."

"No."

"It'll just take a minute."

He was still trying to say no when Jeannie and Rubylee piled out of the diner. He tried to say no when they reached the trucks. He tried to say no even after he knew that Jeannie and Rubylee weren't listening anymore.

Jeannie went with Dundee, and Rubylee got into the truck with Miller. He turned the heat on to blow some air over her wet clothes, and they waited while Dundee put some gas in the truck.

Then they made a caravan, the two beat-up trucks carrying four banged-up teenagers to fates none of them were certain of.

33

MILLER LEFT the truck running in front of the house and jumped out. He walked back to Dundee in the truck behind him and made a cranking motion.

Dundee rolled his window down and Miller pointed to one side of the washed-out gravel drive. "Park it there. Turn around so you're facing out."

Dundee flicked a fast finger salute and spun the wheel.

Miller went back to his truck and parked parallel to Dundee so the two made a front facing away from the house.

They all got out and Rubylee said, "You're not going to put it in the barn?"

Jeannie looked at Rubylee.

"He had the truck in the barn. So those men wouldn't see us if they came."

Miller shook his head. "I'm not hiding anymore. They have nothing left to take from us. Those Wilkins or anybody else." He didn't know if it was true, but saying it so he could hear it made it easier to believe. He pulled the rifle from the truck. "Rubylee and Dundee won't be here long. I'm going to finish this, one way or another."

Nobody said anything as they walked to the house. When they reached the porch steps, Miller stopped and said to Jeannie, "I've changed my mind. After you get Rubylee some clothes, you're going with her and Dundee."

"I'm not."

He spun and pushed his face into Jeannie's. "You are. This isn't a game, and you shouldn't be here."

"I can help."

"You can't."

Jeannie jammed both hands into Miller's shoulders and tried to push him back, but his heels were dug in and he leaned into her so she couldn't move him.

"You get Rubylee changed, then you have to go with them."

"You said I could come home with you."

"You did. And now you'll have to go again."

"Asshole."

It was a step up from mental midget. Miller let her have it. She may as well learn to cuss in front of him when she was in the right. He stepped back. "If that's what it takes to get you to go, then I'm an asshole."

They went up.

The house was quiet and empty. Just like a home, their home, waiting for them to step back into it and keep on living in it like nothing had happened.

But things had happened. Ma and pa were gone. They had no way to pay the bills or keep buying food. No way to keep the county folks away. Or the Wilkins.

Miller flicked the switch by the door and the lights came on. It was a relief to see the electricity was still there.

Jeannie took Rubylee to her bedroom to find some clothes that would fit her. Dundee tried to follow them but the girls kicked him out. He looked around trying to find something to do. Miller said, "We could build a fire."

Dundee shrugged. "Could."

"There's some wood outside."

Dundee went to get some.

Miller thought it hadn't been below freezing yet and the pipes shouldn't have frozen. He tried the kitchen tap and water ran. He took a glass from the cabinet and filled it and drank it straight down.

The bowls that Jeannie had laid out with extra food for the dog still lay where he'd left them on the counter. The bowls were long empty, and Bailey had disappeared. It was a wonder the dog wasn't lurking, waiting for the bowls to be filled again.

He rinsed the bowls and wiped them and put them away. He wanted things to feel more normal, wanted to be able to will that to be true. The bowls belonged in the cupboard. He'd put them there. That was more normal.

He heard the girls talking in Jeannie's room and then Dundee came in with his arms full of wood.

Miller reached out to help Dundee. The two had known each other for most of their lives, but they'd never been close or spent much time together. They were awkward and couldn't anticipate each other's moves, and the firewood tumbled to the floor as Miller reached out.

Dundee squatted on his toes. "Sorry." He reached for the logs to gather them.

"It don't matter. Just leave them there. I'm gonna burn it anyway."

Dundee let the wood lay, and Miller set paper and tinder into the stove and laid a fire to kindle.

The boys watched the flames climb in the potbelly chamber. When it was crackling, Miller pushed in more tinder and a couple of split lengths of log.

The heat kicked up.

Dundee watched, then said, "I don't think it's a good idea what you're doing."

"What exactly am I doing?"

Dundee pushed his fingers into his pockets and hesitated before he said it. "Staying here."

"What all else am I supposed to do?"

"There's gonna be some kind of trouble. Y'all can't stay here with neither your ma or your pa around."

Miller gave Dundee a long look.

"How are you going to pay for anything?"

"I bought you a chicken dinner, didn't I?"

Dundee dropped his head. "That won't last long. What about when them county people come back? What're you gonna tell them?"

Miller said nothing.

"What about the Wilkins? If they come back looking for your pa. I see what they did to you last time."

Miller had forgotten the marks on his face. He figured they'd faded. His hand went unconsciously to his chin before he pulled it back down. "You got any better ideas?"

"Wish I did. You could call the police."

Miller let out a snort. "What all d'you think they'd do?"

"Hard to say. I ain't never had much use for the police. Never seen them do much more than sit in their cars and give tickets."

"What all good d'you think they'd be now?"

Dundee toed a piece of firewood on the floor. "You can't work it out on your own. And Jeannie needs…"

It hung unfinished between them, Miller wondering what it was that Dundee thought Jeannie needed. He said, "I figure the police would take me and Jeannie away right quick. Call the county people and that'd be that."

"You'd probably be safe."

"What's that worth if you've got nothing else?"

Dundee's shoulders went up and slumped back down. "I can't say, but it's got to be worth something."

Miller knew it was. And he knew also that safety wasn't enough. He couldn't leave here until he'd fought for what was supposed to be his. And when that thought went through Miller's head, another went with it: that sounded like mountain talk. The way the people in these hills thought and believed. He was one of them. He'd tried to escape it, but it had caught him. He would make his stand here like hillfolk did.

Dundee said, "The county people are going to come and take you anyway."

"I guess they are."

"Better them before the Wilkins. Ain't much sense in staying here and maybe getting yourself killed."

"Why would the Wilkins kill me? It's pa they want."

Dundee pointed to the rifle that Miller had laid across the kitchen table. "You raise that and you know how it could go."

"I guess I do."

"Is that what you want?"

Miller knew the answer. But he didn't say it. He wanted there to be another option, some other truth that would come before the rifle. He didn't say it because he couldn't see one. "I guess I don't."

"Then come on back to the house with us."

Miller's head swung back and forth. "I can't."

Dundee rubbed his brow. "I suppose I might think the same way if it was Rubylee and me."

Miller's eyes flitted toward the other room. "She's not gonna go with you."

"Jeannie?"

Miller nodded.

"I could ask her."

"I suppose you could."

Dundee thought about it. "I don't suppose it'd do any different than when you asked her."

"I don't suppose it would."

The two stood a moment. The stove ticked as it heated up.

Miller said, "Then you'd better get going."

"So that's it then?"

Miller shrugged. He guessed it was.

Dundee said, "You change your mind, you come on over. Pa's gonna be mad out of his mind I run off with the truck, but he won't turn you and Jeannie away if you get into trouble."

"I know it."

Dundee stepped back.

"Dundee?"

He stopped. "Yeah?"

"Thanks."

Then there was nothing left to say, so Dundee went to the bedroom and stood outside the closed door. "You two about ready?"

They came out, Rubylee wearing a pair of Jeannie's jeans and sneakers and a heavy hooded sweatshirt. She looked at Miller. "I left your clothes in there."

"That's fine. You can get your wet things from the truck on your way out."

Rubylee moved toward the door and Dundee followed her. Jeannie did not.

Miller came to Jeannie and took her arm. "You should go with them."

She pulled away. "I won't."

"Jeannie—"

"I'm not going."

"This is not—"

Her tears made him stop. She pushed her face into her hands. "You really are an asshole. You can't make me leave. You're everything I've got left."

His shoulders dropped. And she was all he had.

Jeannie said, "Come with me. Let Anna try to help. Let somebody try. We don't have to do this alone."

Miller put an arm gently around her. They shouldn't have to do this at all. "You're right."

She leaned into him and for a moment they embraced. Miller was acutely aware that Rubylee and Dundee were watching them. He didn't care. It was all bullshit. This hillbilly code. The way men acted. The way he was acting. It was time to stop.

He pulled away from Jeannie. "OK. Let's go."

She sniffed.

"Let's go see if your Anna Bostwick can help us."

"You mean it?"

"I do."

Miller turned them toward the door. He set his mind to what would come next, what he had to do.

That's when they heard the sound of an engine coming up the drive.

34

MILLER WATCHED a black pickup jostle up the muddy pot-holed drive and stop with its nose pointed at the two trucks in front of the house.

Miller knew who would be in the truck before the two men got out. He could see through the window that one of the men had a beard that was crooked and patchy on one side, and the other beside him with stringy hair was the man who'd worn a pistol on his hip. The Wilkins.

Miller stepped to the door and threw the barrel of the slide bolt into the catch. He ran for the kitchen and the rifle on the table there. "Jeannie! Get out the back. Take Rubylee and Dundee and do like I told you. Get into the woods."

They all three looked at him. Miller waved the rifle. "Go!"

Dundee shook his head. Jeannie and Rubylee stepped back but didn't get their jackets or head for the door.

"Go on!"

Dundee crossed to the window and pulled a corner of the curtain back an inch. "Is that the Wilkins?"

"It's them."

"They don't look happy."

Miller grabbed the curtain away from Dundee and let it fall back into place. "This isn't your fight. Take Jeannie and Rubylee and get out of here."

Dundee stepped away and calmly pulled on his jacket. "It's not your fight either. This is stupid. All of it."

Miller didn't disagree.

"You should call the cops. Right now."

"We talked about this."

"And you didn't listen." Dundee reached for the door and drew the bolt back, and before Miller knew what was happening Dundee twisted the knob, opened the door, and stepped through.

Miller's mind spun, trying to catch up. He looked to Jeannie and Rubylee, then turned and followed Dundee out onto the porch, the rifle in his hand.

Dundee was at the rail, hands waist-high resting on the top. Looking relaxed like he was watching the weather or thinking about a girl he knew.

Miller came beside Dundee and stood at the top of the steps facing down at the Wilkins, the rifle in full view. He felt vulnerable and exposed and invigorated at the same time.

The men were standing behind the open doors of the truck, one on each side. Miller could not see their hands or what might have been in them.

Then the long, black barrel of a gun poked through the space between the door and the truck frame where bad-beard hunched. The barrel pointed to Miller's truck. He laughed. "You got clothes hanging in there?"

Miller remembered the men from before. This Wilkins was Virgil. The man who had kicked him when he was down. An anger and indignation rose in him and he fought to control it. "What do you want?"

"Your pa."

"My pa ain't here."

"Says you."

Miller waved the end of the rifle in his hand. "Go on. Get out of here."

Virgil Wilkins spat from behind the truck door. "Boy, you got a mouth."

Miller felt the heat again. "I got more than that."

Virgil's head jerked behind the door. "You better slow down before you get more than you can handle."

"You better get on out of here."

The other brother, Hank, rose up and showed himself behind the truck door's window. "Your pa inside?"

Miller knew he could raise the gun, point it at the man, and get off a shot. Draw blood and maybe kill the man. The anger in him wanted to do it. But he didn't want to be like the men in the hills who turned to their demons and let them loose. He didn't want to slide further down that path of ruin and guilt that already ate at him for what he'd done to the Bowmans.

And he didn't want to draw fire to himself and Dundee. To leave Jeannie and Rubylee to what the men would do if he couldn't stand in front of them.

Miller raised his chin and answered the man. "My pa was home, you'd be full of holes by now."

Hank scooted down behind the truck door. A shotgun came up around the window.

Miller squinted. "That my shotgun?" The gun they'd taken from him when they were here before.

"Was."

"I'll have it back. Then you can leave."

Miller was within range, and so was Dundee. A blast from the shotgun wouldn't take them to pieces all at once, but it would take enough that it would be the end. He raised his voice. "I told you my pa ain't here. You got no call to come here."

"I think you know where your pa is."

"He's dead."

"We'll just come in and have a look-see. Set that rifle down and step back from it."

Miller stood his ground.

"This don't have to hurt any more than necessary."

"You go on."

Hank stepped from behind the truck door, Miller's shotgun leveled in his hands. "Put the rifle down. You ain't gonna shoot me."

Miller didn't know. He didn't know if he would shoot.

Hank took a step forward and the door behind Miller opened and Jeannie stepped out.

"No!"

"Did you say pa is dead?"

"Jeannie, get back inside."

Dundee was moving now, stepping in front of Jeannie, between her and the men. "Go on back in."

Jeannie shoved Dundee and ducked around him. She leaned out over the rail and shouted, "My daddy would chew your arm off and stuff it up your ass."

Dundee grabbed Jeannie, trying to pull her from the rail, but she struggled and hung on.

Miller wondered what desperation in Jeannie had made her say such a thing, and he figured it was the same that was coursing through him.

The men advanced now, slowly and side-by-side. Miller noticed a bobble in Virgil's step.

Jeannie stopped struggling and Dundee let her go. Then the front door opened again and Rubylee came out beside Jeannie. Both girls stood at the rail and faced the men coming at them.

Dundee moved beside his sister until the four of them on the porch made a line against the Wilkins.

Virgil and Hank Wilkins stopped at the bottom of the steps and looked up. Hank squared his eyes on Miller. "I don't think your pa is here." He put a boot onto the first step up. "No, I don't think Zebulon would be chicken-shit enough to send his kids out to fight for him."

Miller didn't move or speak. None of the others stirred.

Hank pointed a knobby finger at Jeannie. "Missy, you got some lip on you. Didn't your mamma teach you how to be a lady?"

"My mamma taught me a lot of things, but—"

Miller put a hand out in from of Jeannie. "Stop." He turned to the men. "Our pa ain't here. Get on your way."

Hank's eyes narrowed. "Virgil, you hear that? This boy tellin' us to go."

"I heard it."

"And we ain't got what we came for yet."

Virgil cocked a hip with the rifle laid across it. "But we aim to."

Miller fingered the rifle in his hand, thinking about how fast he could pull the barrel up, draw a true bead. How it would feel when his finger pressed into the trigger. "Jeannie. Get inside. Take Rubylee."

No one of them moved.

Hank rocked forward on his boot against the step. "You know why we're here?"

"I know."

"Your daddy killed my kin."

Miller said nothing. He let them think it was his pa had killed the Bowmans.

Hank squinted. "I think you know where your pa is."

Miller's fingers twitched on the butt and the trigger of the rifle. "My pa is dead."

"He ain't dead because we ain't killed him yet."

Miller tried to wish the others off the porch. Then he tried to wish himself away. It came to nothing.

Hank rocked again on the bottom step. "Where you hiding him?"

"Nowhere."

Another rock back and forward. "Out back in the barn?"

"No." Miller's fingers tightened. He didn't fight them.

"Out in them woods somewhere?" Another rock back and forward.

"No."

"Where!" Hank Wilkins leaned up the steps toward Miller.

Miller stood his ground. Dundee was a rock beside him. Jeannie and Rubylee were statues.

"Boy, you tell me where he is or I'll wring your neck."

Hank took one more step up. Miller raised the rifle, the barrel angled down a few feet in front of the man.

Hank swatted but didn't reach the gun. "Put that damn thing down."

Miller racked the bolt back and forward to chamber a load.

Hank twitched. Rubbed his chin and toyed with the shotgun in his hand. "Goddammit!" It came out a high, shrill call and Hank shuddered. "Virgil. Get around back."

Virgil staggered. Miller thought now that the man looked drunk, and wondered if he was.

Hank stepped back from the porch and squared himself some small distance back.

Virgil ran off around the house.

Hank stared at Miller and Dundee and Jeannie and Rubylee up on the porch, and the four of them stared back. A cold wind raised itself and swirled around the menagerie. No one gave the wind its due.

Miller's hand ached from the pressure he kept on the stock of the rifle. He loosened his grip the smallest amount he could. "Dundee. Any chance you can get Jeannie and Rubylee out of here?"

Dundee came behind Miller. Miller moved to let the others pass down the steps. Before they could get through, Virgil stumbled back with a rusted red gas can in his hand. The gas for the chainsaw. The can that Miller had left by the woodpile.

Virgil advanced with the can.

Miller knew that everything had not been taken from them yet. There was more they could lose.

Virgil tipped the can. "Your pa's in there, we'll burn him out." He splashed gas onto the wooden deck. "If he ain't, you'll tell us where he is or we'll burn you to the ground."

Hank had watched. Now he pointed to Dundee. "You bring those girls down off that porch."

Jeannie and Rubylee let Dundee steer them onto the stairs.

Virgil splashed more gas from the can.

Dundee and the girls took a step down.

Virgil cackled.

Miller raised the rifle to his hip.

Hank kept his eyes on Miller and leveled the shotgun.

Dundee and Rubylee and Jeannie went down another step.

Virgil tossed the can onto the porch. It spun and splashed and bounced.

Rubylee ran down the last step and tripped at the bottom.

Hank came forward and held up a silver lighter in his hand. "Where's your pa?"

Dundee bent to lift his sister. Jeannie bumped into Dundee from behind and they both stumbled over.

Hank shouted up at the barrel of the rifle Miller held on him. "Where is he?"

Miller felt as if he was floating away. He felt his finger on the trigger, wanted to pull it but couldn't in his floating state. He felt everything slipping away. He was ready to let go. He was ready to kill another man.

There was a sound, a rustling and scrabbling, and Miller felt himself coming back and then there was teeth and fur and Hank going over backward, the silver lighter falling away with his hand.

There was Bailey slashing into Hank and Hank pulling away and Bailey's grip sinking deeper into Hank's arm. The shotgun was gone now, Miller's shotgun, fallen away as Bailey jerked and shook his head and Hank retreated.

Then Virgil screaming wickedly and drunkenly and coming at them. Coming at Miller and Hank and Bailey and the mess of Jeannie and Rubylee and Dundee still tangled from their fall.

Virgil lunged and Miller leaped. He flipped the rifle in his hand and swung hard from the barrel, and there was a crack as the stock hit Virgil's head and the man went down.

Miller's body shook with something he could barely control. He bent and picked up his shotgun that Hank Wilkins had dropped. Then he whistled and called out to his dog. "Bailey! Down!"

The dog eased but did not let go of Hank's arm.

"Bailey!"

The dog let go and then it was over. The man retreated and cradled his arm.

Miller pumped the shotgun and put the barrel on Hank. "You son of a bitch."

He felt the rage in his head, in his hand, in his finger on the gun's trigger. He felt it all, and he was ready to let it go.

And as he balanced there between one decision and the next, he heard an engine whine and saw in the periphery of his vision a truck veer from the road and careen over the broken terrain toward the house at high speed.

35

MILLER THOUGHT a man Rebel's size shouldn't be able to move that fast, but Rebel did.

Rebel's big arms had Hank Wilkins wrapped up, Hank howling and holding his bitten hand and not putting up much of a fight. Rebel twisted Hank and reached to the man's waist, felt around and pulled out the pistol Hank had tucked there. Rebel tossed the gun onto the porch and pushed Hank Wilkins away.

Virgil was on his feet but unsteady, one hand to his head and the other fluttering like it didn't know where to go. He stumbled and tried to kick at Bailey, who snapped at his feet.

Rebel took charge. He planted a leg behind Hank and scooped the man down to the ground. "Jeannie, come get this dog!"

Then Rebel moved to Virgil and he held the man up to keep him steady. "What else?"

Virgil understood what that meant and shook his head.

Rebel shoved Virgil's arms up and reached around under the man's coat. He came up with no other weapons, and when Rebel let go of Virgil, Miller thought for a moment that the man might fall down and puke. Virgil did neither. Instead he leaned against the porch and glared, the patchy beard on half his face showing ragged scars beneath.

Bailey growled and fought against Jeannie, but she worked the dog back to the porch.

Rebel stepped back. "This stops now."

Hank came to his feet and faced Rebel.

Rebel said, "These kids' pa is dead. You got no more call to come here or give them trouble."

Hank gripped his injured hand and pulled the sleeve of his shirt down against the blood. "It's done when I say it's done."

"Zeb Brenning is dead."

"I'll believe that when I see it myself."

Rebel held Hank's gaze. "You know who I am?"

Hank nodded. "I figure you'd be Rebel Martin."

"And I know for damn sure you're Hank and Virgil Wilkins." He looked from one man to the other. "Though I can't say I know which of you is which."

Virgil moved forward. Rebel let him but kept a close eye. "I'm Virgil."

Rebel nodded.

"And I ain't seen Zebulon's dead body neither." Virgil was wobbly but looked mean enough to overcome it.

Miller came forward. "Rebel."

Rebel looked up at Jeannie and Rubylee and Dundee who had gone back up onto the porch. Dundee had the rifle and pistol Rebel had taken from the Wilkins.

Rebel said, "Which one is Jeannie?"

Jeannie leaned out over the porch rail. "Me."

"I haven't seen you since you was this high." He put a hand at his waist.

Jeannie said, "I remember."

"Who are them others?"

Jeannie pointed. "That's Rubylee Slocum. And her brother Dundee."

"What are they doing here?"

Jeannie looked at Miller, but Miller didn't know what to tell her. Jeannie shrugged. "It's kind of a long story."

Rebel nodded. "I'm sorry I had to tell you your daddy's dead like that."

Jeannie's chin bobbed once. "I guess it's not a surprise."

Virgil was next to Hank now and the two men looked more steady, though Hank was inspecting the bites on his hand more closely.

Miller wanted to end this before the Wilkins got their starch back. "Rebel." He came around beside his pa's cousin. The fire in him had cooled some, and a cold truth was taking its place. "We can't just let them go."

Rebel raised a brow.

"They'll just keep coming back."

"I told them your father is dead. This is over."

Hank released the hand he'd been holding and flexed a finger as if to determine if it would still work. "The boy's right."

Miller traded the rifle in his hands for the shotgun in Dundee's. He felt the heft of the stock and lifted the sights up level.

Rebel laid a hand on the gun. "Now hold on."

Virgil scratched the patchy spaces on his chin where the beard wouldn't grow, digging a finger down into the scars. "You run us off and we'll come back. You kill us, our kin will come. Wilkins will haunt this place until Zebulon pays for the blood he's spilled."

Rebel pushed down the barrel of the shotgun Miller held. Then Rebel looked Virgil square in the eye. "Zeb's dead. There ain't no more debt to pay."

Virgil spat. "I'll believe that when I see it."

Rebel stared at Virgil for a long time, and Miller wondered if Rebel might strike the man or do worse.

Miller's fingers twitched around the shotgun's finger guard. He felt trapped. An anger would not let him go. He felt trapped by the rage of these men. By the rage his pa had lived and created and passed down to him. Trapped by the code of these hills. By inertia and mud and blood and loss.

There was no way out. He could kill, but that would sink him deeper into the dark cycle of ugliness. If they let Hank and Virgil go, the men would come back. The trap would be sprung, over and again, the vicious teeth biting and biting again.

Miller looked at Rebel. "How do you know pa's dead?"

"It don't matter."

"It does. How do you know?"

It caught the Wilkins' attention. Miller watched them waiting for the answer.

Rebel let it sit between all of them for a minute. Then some mechanism in his mind cleared and he said, "Quirt Aikins."

It meant nothing more to Miller than when he'd heard the name before, but both Wilkins jerked.

Hank wagged his head. "A cop told you?"

"No. Quirt told me who to ask."

Hank snorted. "What's that mean? I don't trust no police."

Rebel frowned. "Quirt knows where Zeb lays. And he aims to prove it. But police have to move in certain ways. He can't go there yet."

"Police is as rot as anyone."

"Maybe."

Hank stared. Virgil scratched. Hank said, "Who done it? Who killed Zebulon?"

"That I don't know."

Everyone stared. Miller felt an itch at his back as he thought about Jeannie and Rubylee and Dundee behind him. Bailey whimpered. Miller looked over his shoulder and saw Jeannie holding onto the dog as it wiggled and tried to get away. Dundee watched over everything with the rifle in his hands, like a sentinel, but without direction.

Rebel said, "Does it matter? Who killed Zeb?"

Hank said, "Not so much as that he's dead."

"And you'll put this to rest? If you see Zeb's body. You'll leave these kids be?"

"We'll let it all be if Zeb is dead."

Rebel ran a rough hand over his chin. "That I can show you."

Both Wilkins grinned.

"It won't be easy."

Hank put a hand out. The hand without the wound. "I'll

have my pistol back."

Miller shook his head.

Hank leaned to Miller's ear. "You want to end this, you're going to have to end it. And we'll do it on even ground. I'll have my pistol back."

Miller looked at Dundee on the porch.

Dundee held up the pistol and the rifle that were the Wilkins'.

Miller waved Dundee down, and Dundee came with the weapons and stood beside Miller. "You sure?"

"I ain't. But I don't guess there's any other way." He guessed he should see what Rebel had to say about it, but Miller didn't. He stepped back from Dundee. "Go ahead."

The Wilkins took their guns. Hank held the pistol awkwardly in his bitten hand. Virgil took the rifle but didn't look any more sober with it than when they'd arrived.

Rebel pointed at Hank's hand. "You want to get cleaned up?"

"No need." Hank took a weathered leather glove from his pocket and pulled it on over the punctures.

The glove fit tight and Miller figured it would staunch the blood. He didn't figure the glove would be easy to get off or that it would do much against the dirt and slobber that Bailey had deposited into the wounds, and he didn't care.

Jeannie started down from the porch. "I'm coming."

Miller shook his head. "You're not."

She stopped and eyed Miller but said nothing. Then she went back up onto the porch.

Miller said to Dundee, "You'll stay with them?"

"I will."

Something passed between the two young men that Miller didn't fully understand, but he felt it was meaningful. An understanding. A different kind of code than they'd seen playing out here. Something better and more meaningful.

Rebel said to the Wilkins, "The kid will ride with me. You can follow."

Miller didn't argue.

Rebel tipped his head to look up at the sky. It was going to be dark soon. He said to Miller, "We're going to need a shovel, and a lantern."

Miller tried not to show his distaste.

Rebel looked at the wet ground. "And a mattock, if you have it."

36

MILLER SANK onto the truck seat next to Rebel. The rain started again. Rebel put the truck into gear. The windshield streaked with drops.

The shovels and mattock rattled in the bed behind them as they went. Miller had found two digging shovels and the mattock. He also found the old kerosene lantern in the barn, but it was empty of fuel and rusted and hadn't been used for so long that Miller didn't think it was worth fooling with. He'd taken the flashlight from the kitchen cupboard instead.

The Wilkins' truck plodded behind them, like a big, boxy boat in tow, two headlights gleaming in the growing darkness.

Rebel grimaced. "This isn't something I want to do." He twisted his neck to look up at the sky. "Won't be the weather for it either."

They reached the road at the bottom of the drive and Rebel turned left, upslope. He hunched over the wheel. "Ain't none of this right by ol' Zeb."

Miller said nothing. He slumped in the seat and watched the rain and the night come. The curves of the road pulled him left and right as his body shifted against the momentum.

He wanted his mind to go blank. To go blank and to stay blank, for what was to come.

Miller didn't know where they were going, and he didn't ask. Rebel kept them on the main roads, the black truck following behind. Darkness came slowly, then all at once as the clouds became heavier and the beat of the rain on the windshield picked up.

The headlights behind them glinted more sharply in the mirrors. Rebel ticked the wipers up a notch faster and wiped moisture from the windshield with a rag. "This isn't good."

Miller's mouth opened but he didn't find the words. Then they came to him but he kept the thought in his head. What of it exactly wasn't good? It was a senseless question.

Rebel smoked and drove. They passed by dimly lit houses set back from the road. They splashed through dark stretches where rainwater sluiced across the slanted pavement and drained into deep slopes at the berm.

They traveled through a hazy string of lights that marked an enclave that was almost big enough to have a name. A streetlight carved out the shape of an old farmhouse with a slumped porch and a barn behind that was caving in. A river ran behind the structures, glimpses of its rising waters catching in the lights as they passed.

There had been a few cars, but now as Rebel turned onto a narrower road everything else fell away. There was only Miller and Rebel in the truck and the Wilkins following steadily behind as the trees closed around them on the one-lane road.

They wound upward, and the road narrowed more. At a sharp curve, Rebel slowed and turned onto a dirt lane. They passed a tiny old church that was sinking into the ground.

Miller thought he knew where they were generally, but this place was new to him.

Limbs from a tree with branches hanging heavy with rainwater slapped the windshield and broke the silence that had settled there. Then the view opened to an expanse of ground at the top of a hill overlooking what Miller guessed would be fields below.

Rebel stopped, and Miller squinted through the wipers and the rain on the windshield. He saw in the headlights squares and rectangles lurking like watchdogs. Headstones.

Rebel reached to the pocket on his door and pulled out a ragged cap and pulled it low on his head.

They stepped out into the cemetery and faced the Wilkins through the rain. Miller had no cap and the rainwater ran down his face and dripped from his chin.

None of them were dressed for it. Hank Wilkins stood with his head down and the rain battering his back. Virgil didn't look any more sober. He seemed the least bothered by the weather.

Hank came forward. "What the fuck is this?"

Rebel stood with water dripping off his cap. "This is where we end it. This is where Zeb lies."

"We have to do this in the rain?"

"You want to come back and do it another time?"

"I don't want to do it at all."

The rain pattered. Rebel said, "This ends it. You'll do it."
He started for the bed of the truck.

Hank Wilkins spun. "Let me see your hands!"

Rebel put them in the air but continued to the back of
the truck. "I ain't gonna shoot you." He reached into the bed
and Miller heard the rattle of the shovels. Rebel kept one
with a digging blade and held the other out to Miller. "That
mattock won't be much good in the mud. We'll come back
if we need it."

Miller took the shovel and followed Rebel. The Wilkins
fell in behind them. Rebel held the long flashlight and
shined it for what it was worth in the rain.

The cemetery was small. Rebel took them into the
graves and then turned. They walked some more and Rebel
stopped and looked around. He flicked the light. It faded
into the dark.

Hank Wilkins called out, "What're you doing? Turn
around!"

Rebel did. "It's no trick. We've got to find the fresh one."

Miller could make out Hank's injured hand twitching at
his waist, where he knew the pistol was. He pointed the way
they'd come. "Something over there."

They followed Miller and when he was close to where
he'd seen something he stopped and pointed. "Shine the
light over there."

Rebel did, and a low dirt mound the shape of a grave
showed itself like a scar against the ground.

Rebel went forward.

Miller followed. "How'd they get a grave dug for pa and
nobody knew he was dead?"

Rebel took off his cap and held it briefly over his heart. "It's not your pa's grave."

Miller didn't understand. The grave wasn't marked yet with a stone.

Rebel put his cap back on. "They put him in with a fresh one."

Hank Wilkins put a toe to the edge of the mound of dirt. "Zebulon is in there?"

Rebel didn't answer. He gave the flashlight over to Miller and swung the shovel to the muddy mound. He sank the shovel into the mud. It cut in neatly without much effort. The rain rolled down the blade and into the slit that had opened.

Rebel leaned forward and instead of lifting the blade, he bent forward and put his face into his hands. His cap fell off and water ran over him as he stooped in his sorrow.

Miller came to Rebel and picked up the cap from the muddy ground. He held the cap and the flashlight out and motioned Rebel to the side.

Rebel took the cap and light and stepped away, and Miller gripped the shovel handle. He levered it down, bent, and scooped.

The dirt came away in a slippery, watery mass. Miller dropped the mess beside the mound and shoved the blade in again. He tried not to think. When he did, he saw the blade of the shovel slicing into what lay beneath the dirt.

The Wilkins moved a few steps away and hunched beneath a sapling. Without leaves, the branches didn't offer shelter. The brothers stood there anyway. Hank's damaged hand stayed perched on the grip of the pistol at his waist.

Miller looked to Rebel, who stood blank as a shadow. "How d'you know pa is under there?"

"I don't, for sure."

Miller looked to the Wilkins. "What're they gonna do if he's not?"

"Same as before, I suspect."

Miller kept digging.

He'd opened a trench maybe a foot deep at one end of the mound and was struggling to widen the hole when the mud gave way and the side of the hollow collapsed.

Miller dragged the shovel blade through the slush and pulled out a channel at one corner of the mound to let the mud through. The blade caught on something. Rebel saw it and shined the light.

Miller forced his mind to go empty and knelt down into the mud. His hands went in and he pulled away muck and exposed the tip of a boot.

Pa wasn't deep. Left like he was, he might have floated to the surface in the rains. Someone would have found him, or the birds or the woodland creatures.

Miller dug with his hands. He felt the length and direction of the boot, and he raised up and took the shovel again.

He dug gently but quickly at the head of the mound. When he'd made a little progress he dropped to his knees and dug again with his hands.

It didn't take long. A muddied scrap of fabric emerged. Miller worked at it and found the collar of a shirt.

He couldn't stop. If he did he would never start again.

The flashlight wobbled unsteadily in Rebel's hand, and the light dimmed. Miller clawed his fingers into the earth.

He felt a jawline, worked his hands down to shoulders.

He dug, his hands cold and stiff and his body wet and shivering, his mind in a dark and distant place it had never gone before.

The flashlight dimmed again. Rebel tapped the light and shook the handle, and a weak beam came down on the figure emerging from the ground.

Miller pulled mud. He released the top of a head and shoulders.

He dug. He didn't think.

When there was enough room to tilt the head, Miller got the face up out of the mud.

The body didn't look good, mud in the mouth and pushed into the ears. The flesh was mottled and pitted.

The Wilkins came closer. They both leaned into the little glow that still came from the flashlight and lit on the face in the ground.

Hank bent farther forward. "That Zebulon?"

Rebel cleared something from his throat. "That's him."

The rain came steady and surrounded the rotting face, the mud threatening to suck Zeb back down into the ground. Rain washed mud from the brow.

Rebel held the last of the light on the face. "It's Zeb." His voice caught in his throat. "I'll put in a call to Quirt. They'll come out and get the body."

Hank leaned in again. "Well goddam, I ain't never seen nothing like it."

Virgil was already walking away.

Rebel turned the beam of light away from Zeb. "Get the shovels."

Miller did, and they started back. He was muddy and frozen and his mind was overloaded and had pushed him into a dark tunnel.

They left Zeb with his face pushed up out of the ground, his mouth tipped forward like he was trying to take his last drink.

37

MILLER SLOGGED through the cemetery. The Wilkins were already gone when he and Rebel got back to the truck. Miller tossed the muddy shovels into the back and used the bumper to scrape mud from his boots.

The rain beat steady and the dark stayed close. Rebel pulled the driver's door open. "Forget about that."

Miller scraped some more because it gave him something to do that he understood and seemed normal. Then he tried to wipe the grit and mud from his wet pants. The pants streaked and smeared. Miller gave up and bent to wipe his hands on the wet grass.

For a moment, all he thought about was mud. Then an image of his pa's face moldering in the ground came to him, and he felt unsteady and sick.

Miller stood and let the rain fall over him until the nausea and the image passed. Then he climbed into the truck beside Rebel.

The cab was full of smoke. The soggy end of a cigarette

hung from Rebel's lips. He sucked on the butt, stubbed it into the ashtray, and let out a very long exhale.

Rebel looked at Miller as if deciding something, what to say or do next, Miller figured. But Rebel said nothing and started the truck. He ground the gear into reverse and they slipped backward over the wet grass.

They didn't speak on the drive back. Rebel cracked his window and lit another cigarette. He turned the heat and blower up to fight back the cold and wet that had sunk into both of them.

Rebel finished the cigarette and after a few minutes he lit another. Miller's head felt a little light from the fumes. He let the smoke wash over him and tried to forget everything.

There were no vehicles in front of the house when Rebel pulled up. A light glowed from the living room. The rest of the house was dark.

Miller opened his door.

Rebel said, "You sure you don't want you and Jeannie to come with me?"

Miller's throat was tight. He cleared it and said, "No."

"I don't like leaving you alone."

"We been alone before. When it was worse than this. With the Wilkins coming…"

"I guess that's right in one way. But it's worse now in another way."

It was. Miller knew it. "I done all that so we could be here. Me and Jeannie. So we could have our home."

Rebel hunched over the wheel and squeezed it hard under his hands. "I guess you did. But it just doesn't feel right."

Miller slipped a leg out the door. "It isn't right."

"Clean that shovel and put it away."

Miller stepped out into the rain.

"Just…Jesus." The big man lowered his head.

Miller reached into the truck bed and pulled the shovels and mattock out. He tossed them on the ground and waved to Rebel through the window.

The truck backed slowly away and turned around.

Miller washed the tools at the outside spigot and took them back to the barn. He put the padlock on the barn door and walked in the rain to the house.

The light came on when he reached the step. Jeannie held the door open.

Miller came in and worked to pull a wet boot off. "Rubylee and Dundee went home?"

"I asked them to."

Miller worked another boot.

Jeannie said, "It seemed like a family thing."

Miller rolled his socks down and off, thinking about the questions Jeannie would ask in a moment. His feet were wet and cold and wrinkled.

Jeannie said, "There's a fire in the stove."

Miller carried his boots and socks to the kitchen and set them on the floor beside the woodstove. He took his wet jacket off and hung it across the back of a chair. The warmth felt good on his feet and he stretched his toes out to let the heat reach in between them.

Jeannie watched him. Miller wasn't ready. He said, "I'm going to change my clothes."

He came back in a few minutes with dry clothes and wearing his heavy winter socks.

Jeannie stood at the kitchen counter. "You want me to make you some tea?"

"We have tea?"

"I don't know. Mamma used to." She opened a cupboard door and looked in.

"It's OK, I don't want tea."

Jeannie's hands fluttered as she closed the cupboard door.

Something like a stone dropped through Miller's body. "I guess I have to tell you what happened."

Jeannie leaned stiffly against the counter, like a mouse caught looking up at a cat.

Miller rose and took Jeannie's hand in his. "Come on out to the couch."

He led Jeannie to the other room and they settled into their usual spots on the couch. Jeannie reached for the throw on the back and draped it over her shoulders. Her eyes were wide and clear.

Miller sighed and told her. He left the worst of it out, but it was enough.

Jeannie said nothing. Then her face slowly wrinkled. Then she dropped her head to her hands, and then to Miller's lap. She hiccupped and her shoulders bobbed.

Miller put his hand on her back and did his best to think about nothing.

They eventually settled back on the couch, Miller at one end and Jeannie at the other. Their feet overlapped and intertwined in the middle.

Jeannie's eyes were closed for a long time and Miller thought she might be asleep. Then Jeannie's eyes opened and she said, "What happens now?"

"Rebel will tell his friend Quirt. They'll go out and get pa."

It wasn't enough, Miller knew, but Jeannie accepted that and closed her eyes again.

After a few minutes, Miller reached to the light and turned it off. Some time after that, Bailey came in and turned circles on the rug in front of the couch and laid down.

Some time after that, a grayness crept in at the windows. Miller thought he might have slept a little.

The rain had stopped. Bailey was gone. Jeannie was asleep across from him on the couch.

Miller got up and went to the kitchen and relit the fire in the potbelly. Then he put on his still-wet boots and waded out to the woodpile under the lean-to and dug out the Mason jar he'd left there. He took out the forty dollars and tucked it into his pocket.

Some time later, Jeannie woke and he drove them into town. They went into Johnson's Market and he bought them each a hot breakfast sandwich.

They walked past the food barrel and Miller ignored it. He bought bread and eggs and potatoes.

They drove back under clearing skies. When they came around the big slow turn in the flat part of the road that would bring them home, they saw a police car at the house. Mrs. Jackson looked over from the porch next door.

Miller braked. "Make like you don't know."

Jeannie's eyes were wide.

"They can't know you already knew about pa."

The wide went to wet.

"You should go over with Mrs. Jackson."

Miller pulled in away from the police car and went to
talk to the officer. Jeannie walked over to Mrs. Jackson.

The officer held his hat in his hands. "I won't ask where
your mother is. I know she's not here."

Miller didn't answer.

"We don't usually do things this way, but I have a notion
that you already suspect what I'm about to tell you."

Miller nodded.

"Son, we found your daddy."

The officer gave him a very brief version. When he'd
finished, he worried the brim of his hat through his fingers.
"We can't let you and your sister stay here."

Miller turned and walked toward Mrs. Jackson's. The officer followed. Miller was fast and reached the porch before
the officer caught him with a hand on his shoulder.

The door opened and Mrs. Jackson stepped out. Jeannie
was at her hip.

Mrs. Jackson had a phone in her hand. Miller recognized that the phone was his. Mrs. Jackson held her arm out.
"Jed, you'd better take this."

The officer took the phone and talked for a long time, and
Miller wondered that his phone didn't run out of minutes.

Then the officer went to his car and talked on his radio
for a long time. Miller eyed Jeannie.

Jeannie said, "Just wait."

Finally the officer came back to Miller and Jeannie and
Mrs. Jackson. He tapped his hat in his hands and then set it
back on his head and sighed. "You two can come back to the
house. We'll wait there. Somebody named Anna Bostwick
is on her way to straighten some things out."

It was a long time before Anna Bostwick got there. She broke the rules again and let Miller and Jeannie stay at their home.

It was a big risk for Anna, but Jeannie had softened her. Anna stayed for a long time after the officer left and asked them questions about how they felt and if they had food and heat. She looked around the house and checked in the bedrooms and the bathroom.

Anna promised to be back that evening and left them alone.

Miller and Jeannie were quiet for a long time, and then Jeannie said, "I felt like such a baby. When you had to send me over to Mrs. Jackson's."

"You're not."

They left it at that.

Anna came back before dark and brought hamburger and buns and a can of sloppy joe sauce. Miller cooked the sloppy joes with an onion and made fried potatoes in the skillet, and the three of them ate at the table next to the stove with Bailey waiting for a scrap.

After dinner Anna told them their mamma was coming back in the morning.

Neither Miller nor Jeannie said anything.

Anna frowned. "Your mother left because she thought your father might hurt her. She thought he might hurt her real bad."

Jeannie squirmed. Miller kept his back straight.

"Your mother has been staying with your aunt."

Jeannie said, "Aunt Fish."

Anna nodded. "Does it surprise you that your mother

thought your father might hurt her?" She looked from Jeannie to Miller.

Jeannie said, "We figured he might'a already killed her."

Anna's face clouded and she looked at Jeannie for a long time. Then she stood and picked up the plates and carried them to the sink.

It took a long time to convince Anna to leave them there alone for the night. It was Jeannie who convinced her. Miller didn't pretend to understand how she'd done it.

38

MILLER TOOK Jeannie to the place where he'd left the Bowmans.

To the quarry lake out by the county line. Miller drove them down the remote access road and stopped at a flat spot on a rise above the water.

Below them, the water was black in the moonlight. Miller turned the engine off. "The Bowmans are down there."

Jeannie's eyes scanned the surface below. "In their truck?"

"In their truck."

"They won't float up?"

"They won't. I put the windows up."

Jeannie looked for a long time. "How'd you do it?"

"I left them in the truck. I put it into neutral and pushed it over." His thoughts cast back to that moment. "I locked the doors."

"What'd you do that for?"

He blinked. "So they wouldn't slip out, I guess. I just did."

Jeannie's eyes roamed the water's surface some more.

"Everyone will probably think pa killed the Bowmans."

Miller nodded.

"But you did."

"Let them think it was pa."

"Won't folks wonder who killed pa?"

"Let them."

"The police will probably think it was the Wilkins who done pa."

Miller knew they probably already did. "The Wilkins didn't kill pa. That don't mean they won't get clean of it. We've got to play like we don't know anything. Rebel will say he dug up pa's body with the Wilkins and I wasn't there."

"The Wilkins might say otherwise."

"Let them." He looked at the water below and tried to imagine the future. "Someone will find the Bowmans one day. The water level will go down, or someone will come here swimming. Some way they'll find them. One day."

Jeannie's silhouette in the moonlight looked thin and young and graceful. Miller wondered what she would be like on that day. "You can never tell anyone. Any of it. You have to let on that you didn't know. When they find them."

Jeannie turned her head, and the silhouette went from a shadow of her person to someone whole. "Then why'd you bring me here? If you want me to let on like I don't know?"

Miller breathed deep. "I want you to know. I want you to understand and to put away what's happened in some place in your head that it can't get to you. Some place where you know but where it can heal over."

Jeannie turned and her shadow floated in the dark like she was rising on water. "Seems like you killed the men who killed pa. Them Bowmans. You done what had to be done, and you didn't even know it."

Miller worked hard at his thoughts to anchor himself in the cab of the truck. "Seems like I did. But listen to me. Jeannie, we're not going to be like that. We're going to bury that here. We're going to be different."

Jeannie's shadow thickened. "Different how?"

"I don't know yet, but we will be. It will be better."

"How d'you know?"

"These hills don't make the people who live in them. We don't have to be like everyone else."

Jeannie looked down at the water again. "You say it like it's gonna be easy."

"It's not. It's going to be really hard."

Miller looked through the dark at his sister.

Jeannie looked back. They watched each other for a long time, their eyes adjusting to the dim light and to each other.

Then a corner of Jeannie's mouth moved in the tiniest of twitches. Her voice floated across the space between them so softly that Miller wasn't sure if he heard it or dreamed it. "Doofus."

He knew then that they could do it. That others would not define their legacy. They would break the gossamer strands that bound them invisibly to the sins of their forebearers.

Miller knew.

Hi, there.

Thanks for reading.

Will you indulge me in asking a favor? If there's anything you liked about this book – the characters, plot, dialogue, setting, how the characters interacted – anything at all, would you write that in a review on Amazon?

That will help me to know what people like, and what I should try to write more of.

Thanks again for reading. I deeply appreciate it.

Cheers,
Scott

And hey, if you'd like to see more of my writing, check out the Jackson Flint mystery series and other works at my Amazon page. Thanks!

Made in the USA
Coppell, TX
16 December 2022

89712506R10154